Romeo & Juliet

WILLIAM SHAKESPEARE

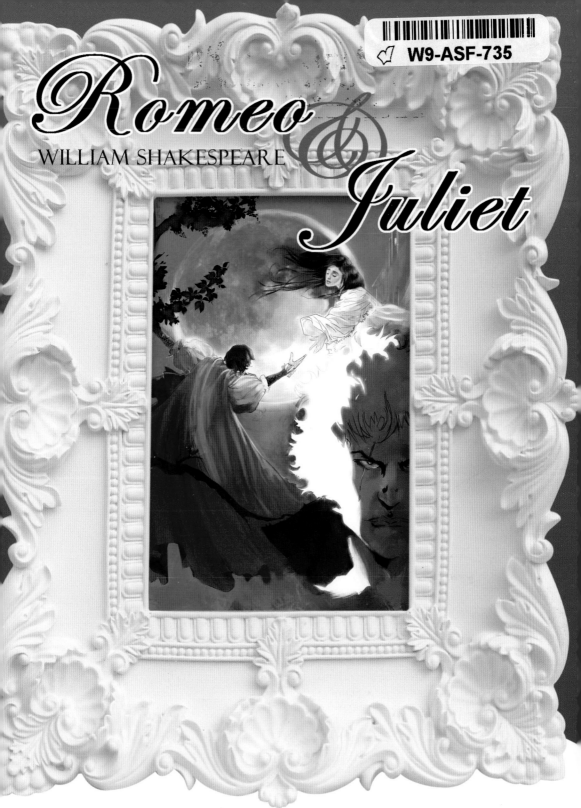

CAMPFIRE™

KALYANI NAVYUG MEDIA PVT. LTD.
New Delhi

Sitting around the Campfire, telling the story, were:

Wordsmith	:	John F. McDonald
Illustrator	:	Sachin Nagar
Colorist	:	Prince Varghese
Letterer	:	Bhavnath Chaudhary
Editors	:	Divya Dubey
		Aditi Ray
Editor (Informative Content)	:	Rashmi Menon
Art Director	:	Rajesh Nagulakonda
Production Controller	:	Vishal Sharma

Cover Artists:

Illustrator	:	Sachin Nagar
Designer	:	Jayakrishnan K. P.

Published by Kalyani Navyug Media Pvt. Ltd.
101 C, Shiv House, Hari Nagar Ashram
New Delhi 110014
India
www.campfire.co.in

ISBN: 978-93-80028-58-3

Printed in India at Rave India

About the Author

Famously known as 'The Bard of Avon', William Shakespeare was born in Stratford-upon-Avon, most probably on April 23, 1564. We say probably because till date, nobody has conclusive evidence for Shakespeare's birthday.

His father, John Shakespeare, was a successful local businessman and his mother, Mary Arden, was the daughter of a wealthy landowner. In 1582, an eighteen-year-old William married an older woman named Anne Hathaway. Soon, they had their first daughter, Susanna and later, another two children. William's only son, Hamnet, died at the tender age of eleven.

Translated into innumerable languages across the globe, Shakespeare's plays and sonnets are undoubtedly the most studied writings in the English language. A rare playwright, he excelled in tragedies, comedies, and histories. Skillfully combining entertainment with unmatched poetry, some of his most famous plays are *Othello, Macbeth, A Midsummer Night's Dream, Romeo and Juliet,* and *The Merchant of Venice,* among many others.

Shakespeare was also an actor. In 1599, he became one of the partners in the new Globe Theatre in London and a part owner of his own theater company called 'The Chamberlain's Men'—a group of remarkable actors who were also business partners and close friends of Shakespeare. When Queen Elizabeth died in 1603 and was succeeded by her cousin King James of Scotland, 'The Chamberlain's Men' was renamed 'The King's Men'.

Shakespeare died in 1616. It is not clear how he died although his vicar suggested it was from heavy drinking.

The characters he created and the stories he told have held the interest of people for the past 400 years! Till date, his plays are performed all over the world and have been turned into movies, comics, cartoons, operas, and musicals.

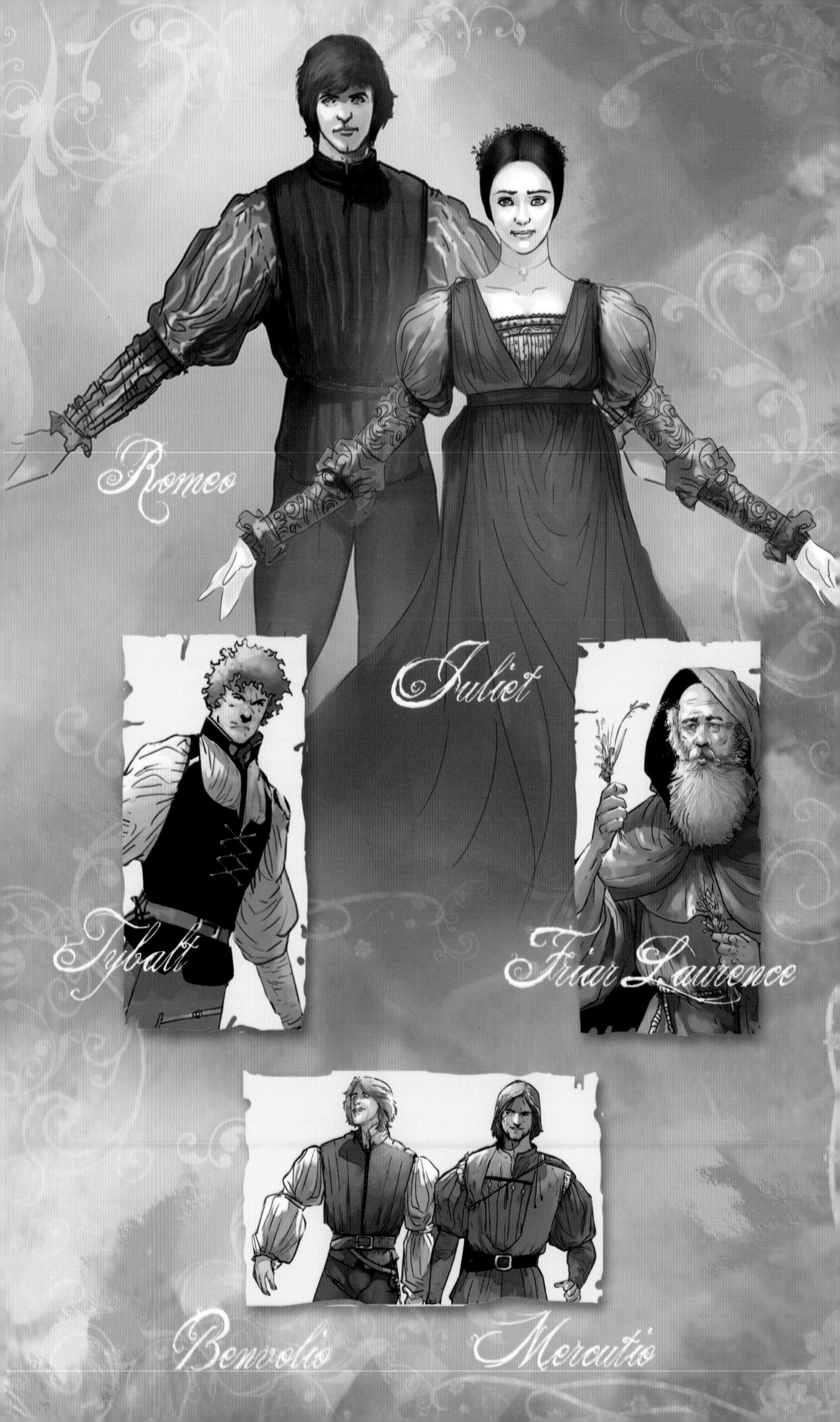
Romeo
Juliet
Tybalt
Friar Laurence
Benvolio
Mercutio

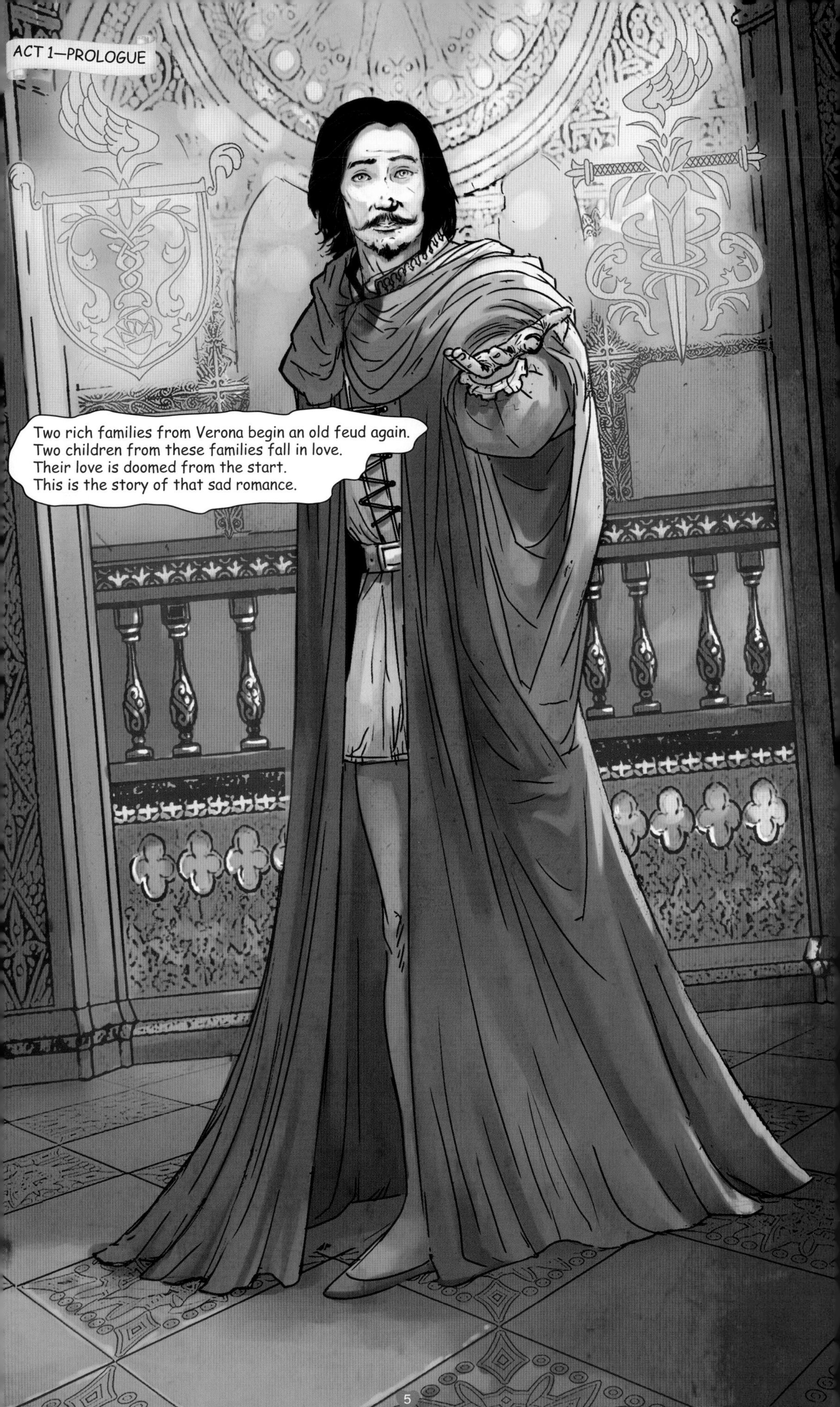
ACT 1—PROLOGUE
Two rich families from Verona begin an old feud again.
Two children from these families fall in love.
Their love is doomed from the start.
This is the story of that sad romance.

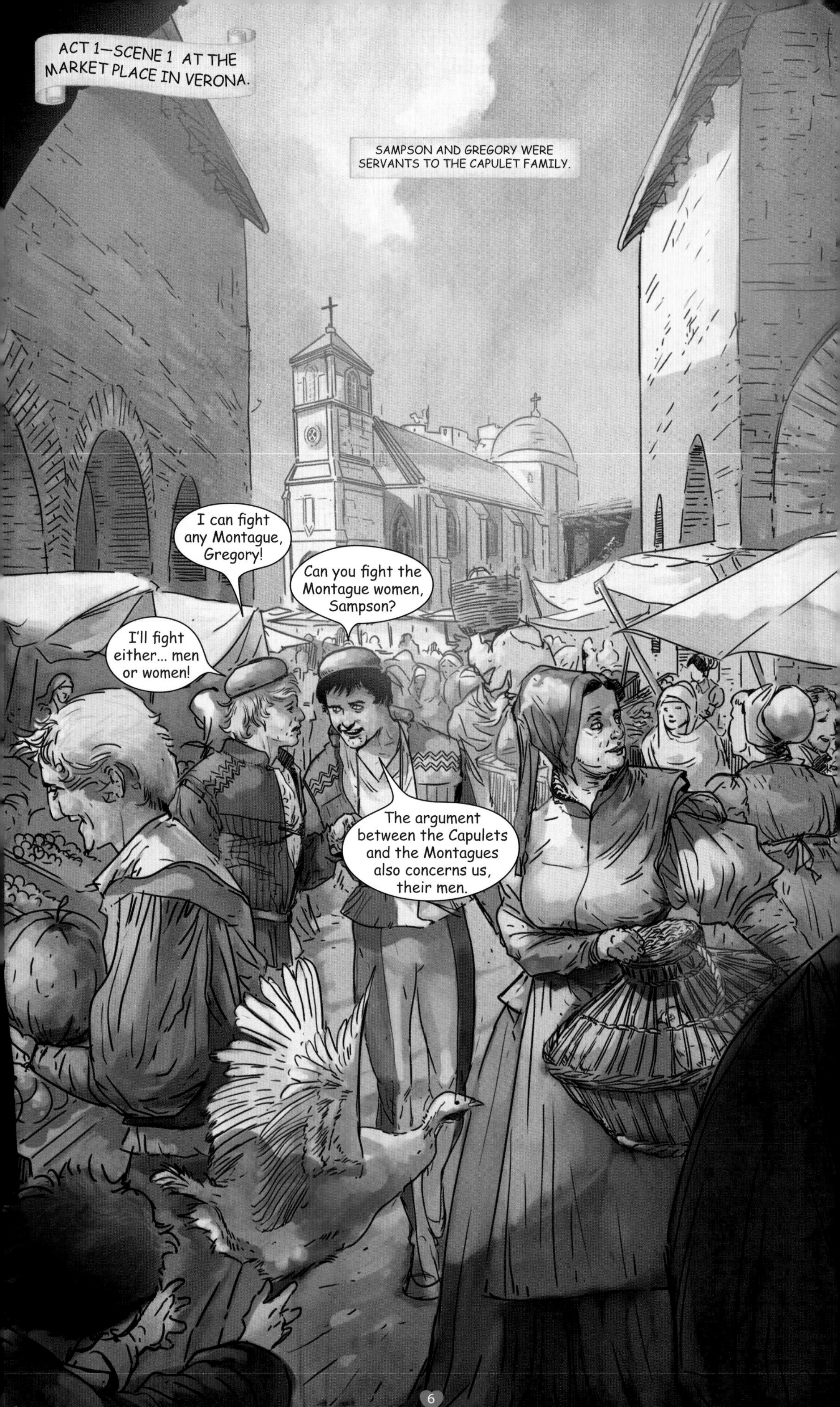
ACT 1—SCENE 1 AT THE MARKET PLACE IN VERONA.
SAMPSON AND GREGORY WERE SERVANTS TO THE CAPULET FAMILY.
I can fight any Montague, Gregory!
Can you fight the Montague women, Sampson?
I'll fight either... men or women!
The argument between the Capulets and the Montagues also concerns us, their men.

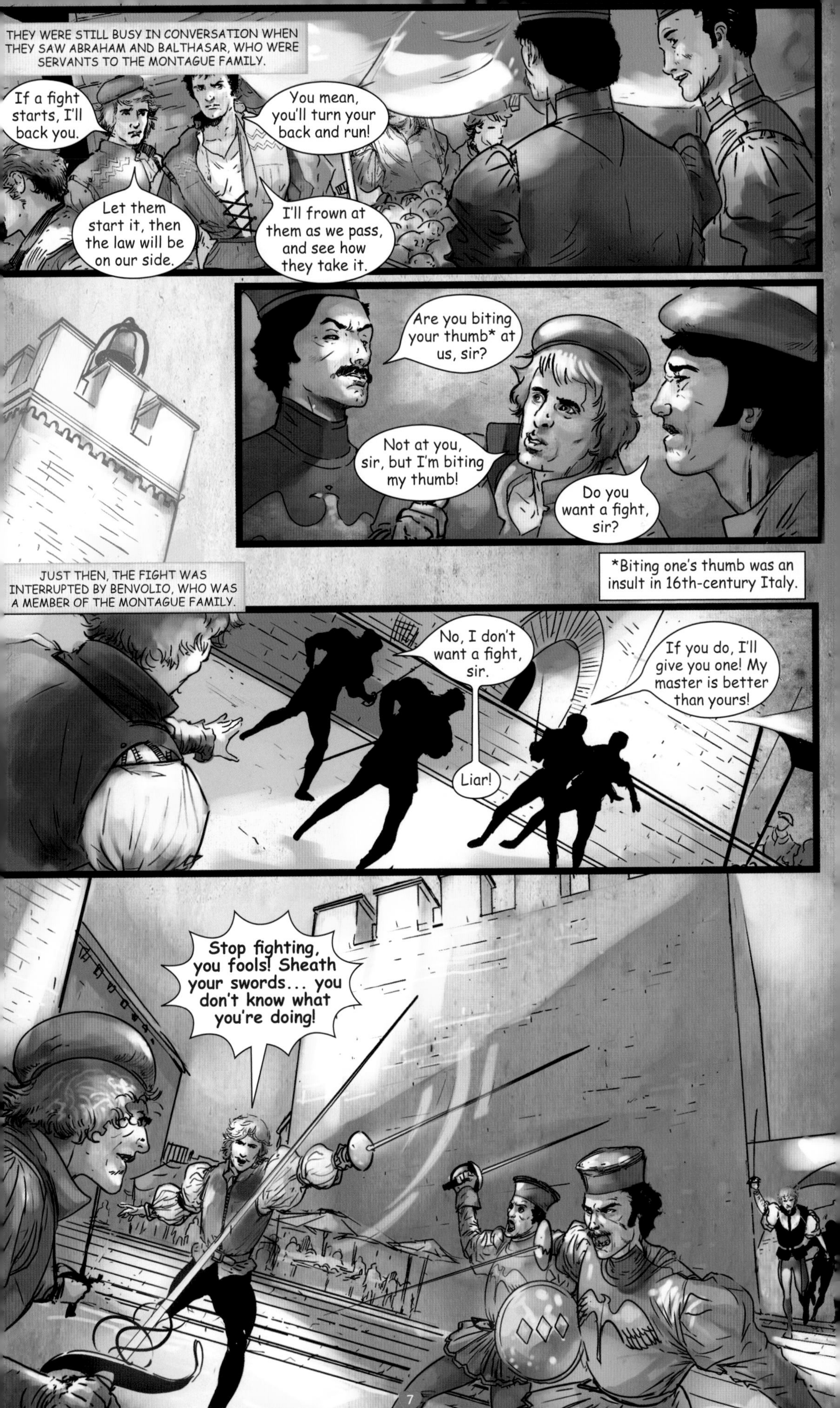

THEY WERE STILL BUSY IN CONVERSATION WHEN THEY SAW ABRAHAM AND BALTHASAR, WHO WERE SERVANTS TO THE MONTAGUE FAMILY.
If a fight starts, I'll back you.
You mean, you'll turn your back and run!
Let them start it, then the law will be on our side.
I'll frown at them as we pass, and see how they take it.
Are you biting your thumb* at us, sir?
Not at you, sir, but I'm biting my thumb!
Do you want a fight, sir?
JUST THEN, THE FIGHT WAS INTERRUPTED BY BENVOLIO, WHO WAS A MEMBER OF THE MONTAGUE FAMILY.
*Biting one's thumb was an insult in 16th-century Italy.
No, I don't want a fight, sir.
Liar!
If you do, I'll give you one! My master is better than yours!
Stop fighting, you fools! Sheath your swords... you don't know what you're doing!

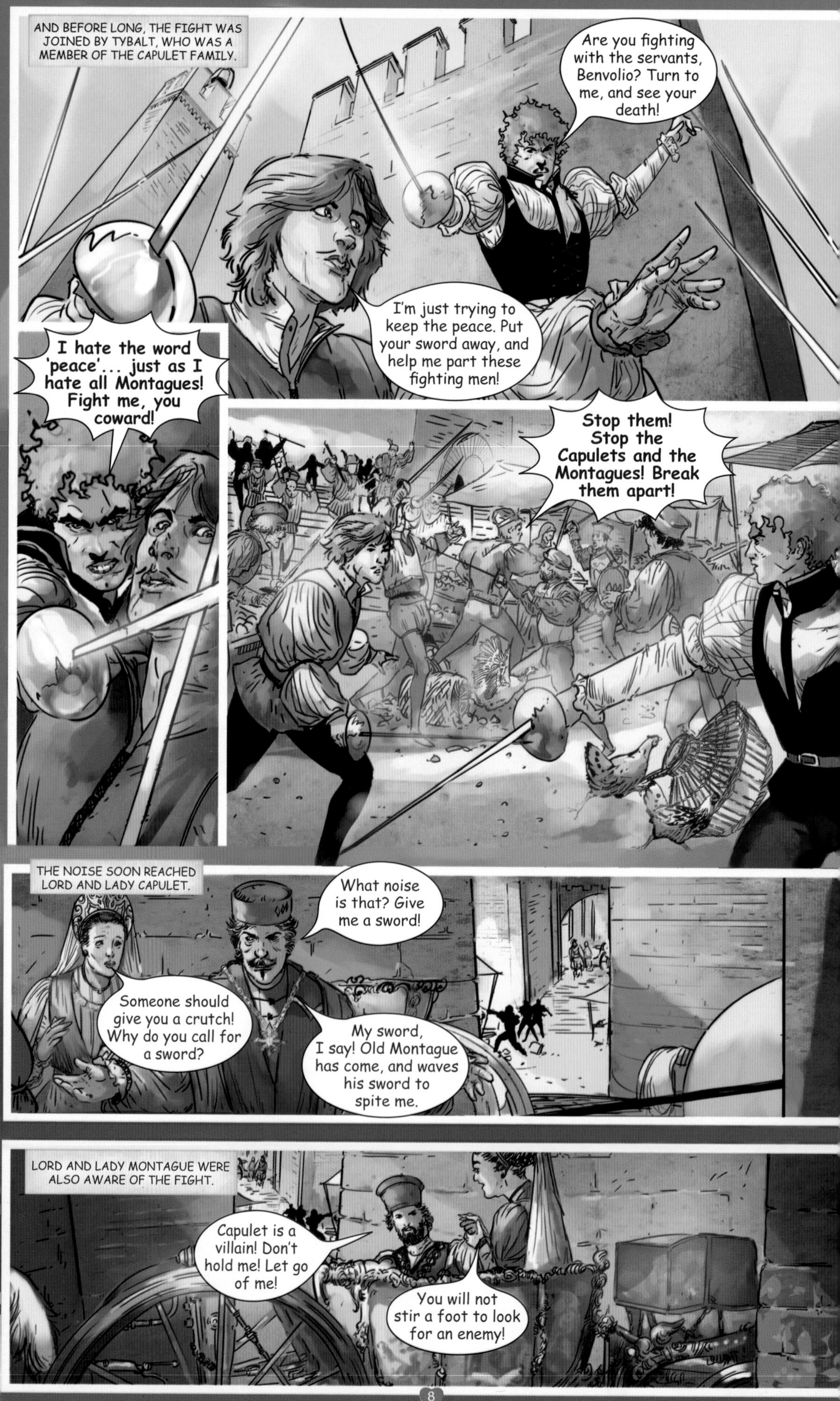
AND BEFORE LONG, THE FIGHT WAS JOINED BY TYBALT, WHO WAS A MEMBER OF THE CAPULET FAMILY.
Are you fighting with the servants, Benvolio? Turn to me, and see your death!
I'm just trying to keep the peace. Put your sword away, and help me part these fighting men!
I hate the word 'peace'... just as I hate all Montagues! Fight me, you coward!
Stop them! Stop the Capulets and the Montagues! Break them apart!
THE NOISE SOON REACHED LORD AND LADY CAPULET.
What noise is that? Give me a sword!
Someone should give you a crutch! Why do you call for a sword?
My sword, I say! Old Montague has come, and waves his sword to spite me.
LORD AND LADY MONTAGUE WERE ALSO AWARE OF THE FIGHT.
Capulet is a villain! Don't hold me! Let go of me!
You will not stir a foot to look for an enemy!

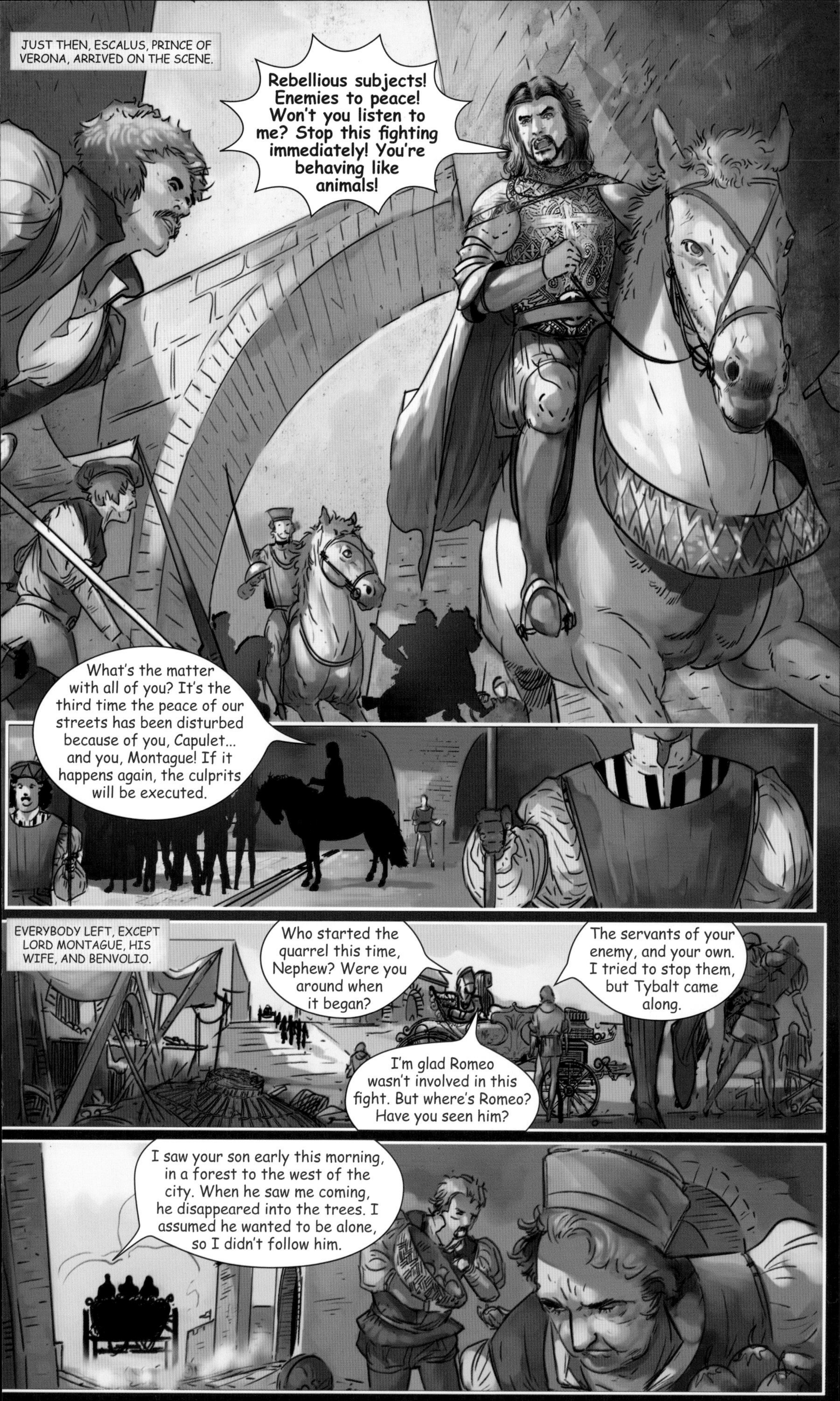
JUST THEN, ESCALUS, PRINCE OF VERONA, ARRIVED ON THE SCENE.
Rebellious subjects! Enemies to peace! Won't you listen to me? Stop this fighting immediately! You're behaving like animals!
What's the matter with all of you? It's the third time the peace of our streets has been disturbed because of you, Capulet... and you, Montague! If it happens again, the culprits will be executed.
EVERYBODY LEFT, EXCEPT LORD MONTAGUE, HIS WIFE, AND BENVOLIO.
Who started the quarrel this time, Nephew? Were you around when it began?
The servants of your enemy, and your own. I tried to stop them, but Tybalt came along.
I'm glad Romeo wasn't involved in this fight. But where's Romeo? Have you seen him?
I saw your son early this morning, in a forest to the west of the city. When he saw me coming, he disappeared into the trees. I assumed he wanted to be alone, so I didn't follow him.

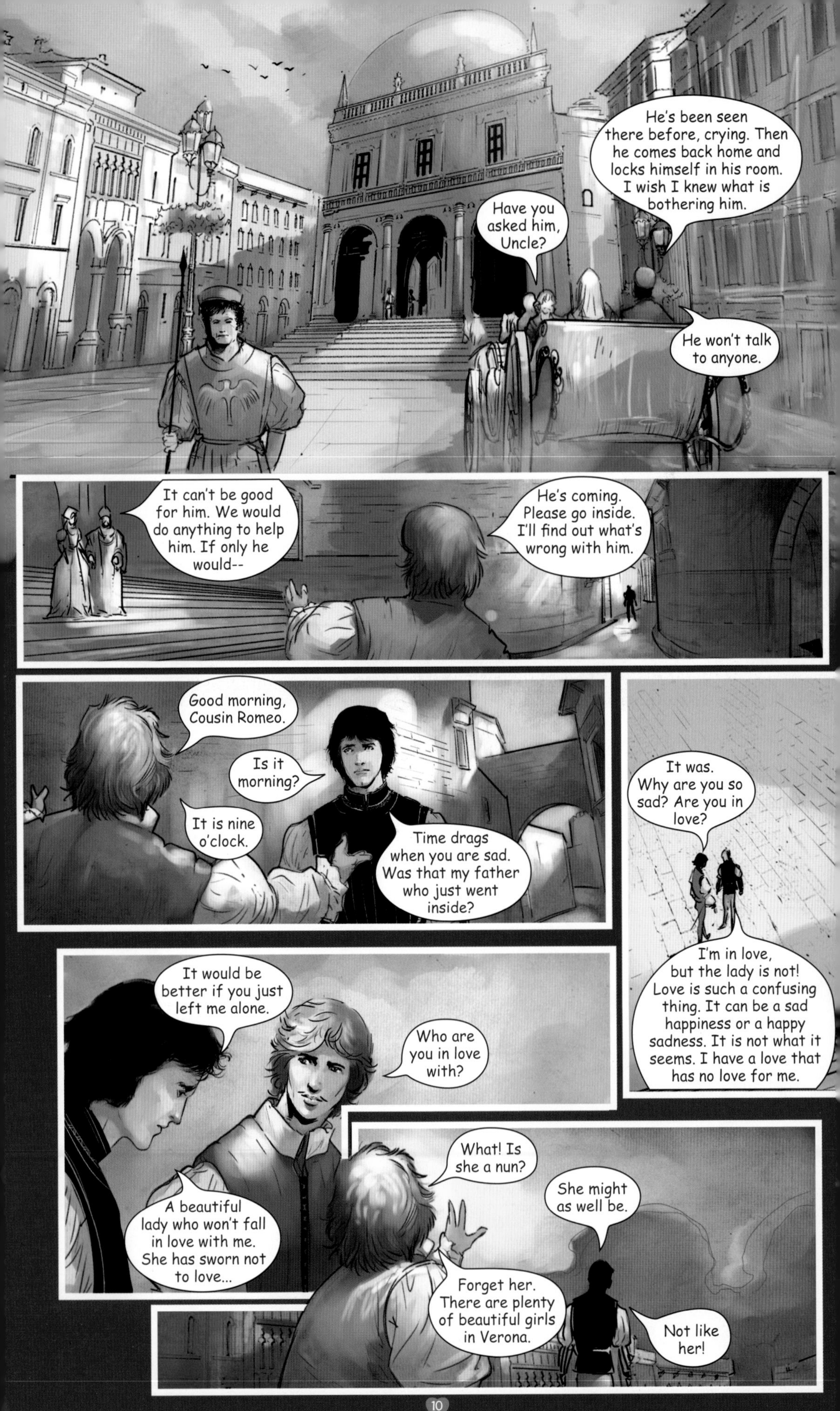
Have you asked him, Uncle?
He's been seen there before, crying. Then he comes back home and locks himself in his room. I wish I knew what is bothering him.
He won't talk to anyone.
It can't be good for him. We would do anything to help him. If only he would--
He's coming. Please go inside. I'll find out what's wrong with him.
Good morning, Cousin Romeo.
Is it morning?
It is nine o'clock.
Time drags when you are sad. Was that my father who just went inside?
It was. Why are you so sad? Are you in love?
I'm in love, but the lady is not! Love is such a confusing thing. It can be a sad happiness or a happy sadness. It is not what it seems. I have a love that has no love for me.
It would be better if you just left me alone.
Who are you in love with?
A beautiful lady who won't fall in love with me. She has sworn not to love...
What! Is she a nun?
She might as well be.
Forget her. There are plenty of beautiful girls in Verona.
Not like her!

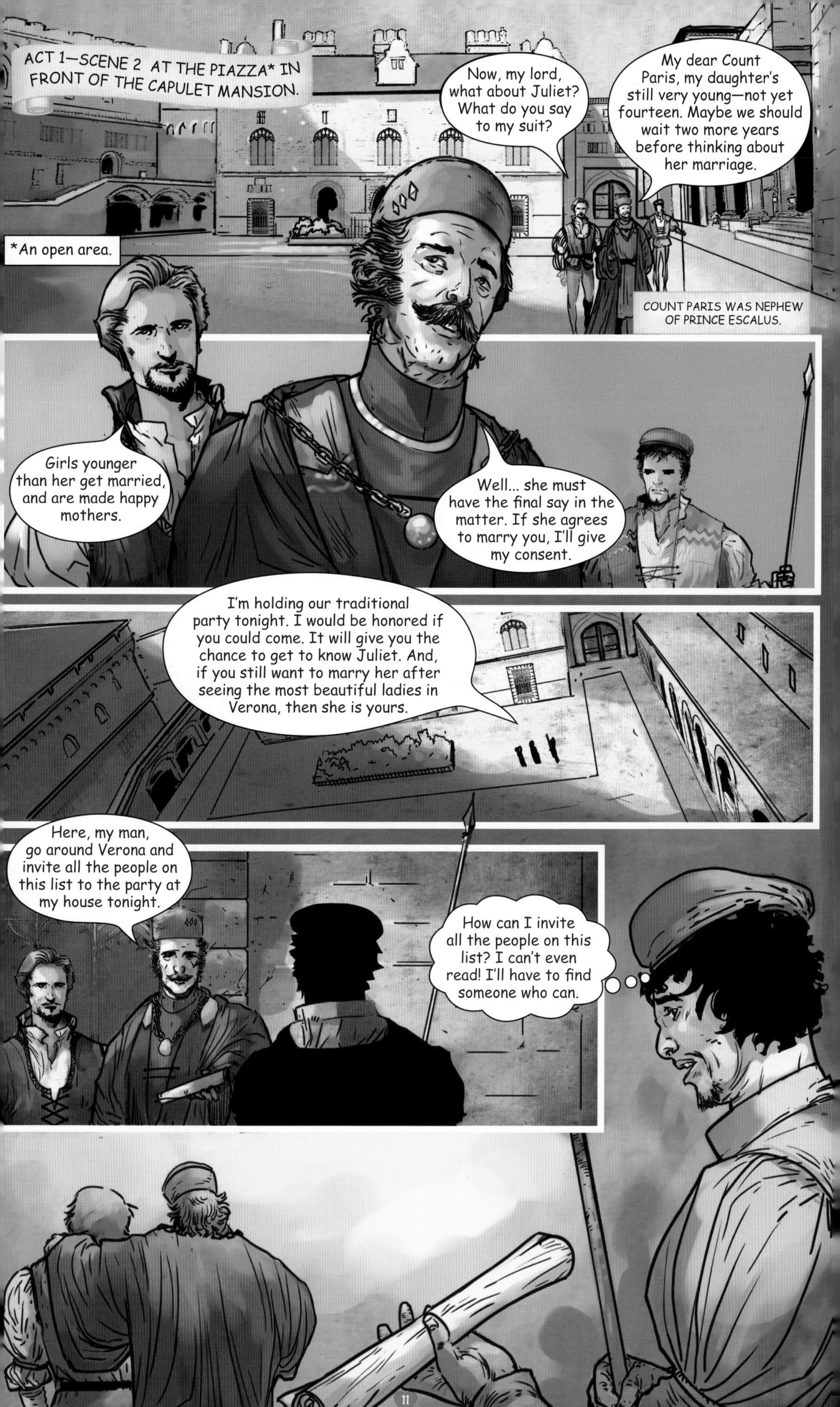
ACT 1—SCENE 2 AT THE PIAZZA* IN FRONT OF THE CAPULET MANSION.
*An open area.
Now, my lord, what about Juliet? What do you say to my suit?
My dear Count Paris, my daughter's still very young—not yet fourteen. Maybe we should wait two more years before thinking about her marriage.
COUNT PARIS WAS NEPHEW OF PRINCE ESCALUS.
Girls younger than her get married, and are made happy mothers.
Well... she must have the final say in the matter. If she agrees to marry you, I'll give my consent.
I'm holding our traditional party tonight. I would be honored if you could come. It will give you the chance to get to know Juliet. And, if you still want to marry her after seeing the most beautiful ladies in Verona, then she is yours.
Here, my man, go around Verona and invite all the people on this list to the party at my house tonight.
How can I invite all the people on this list? I can't even read! I'll have to find someone who can.

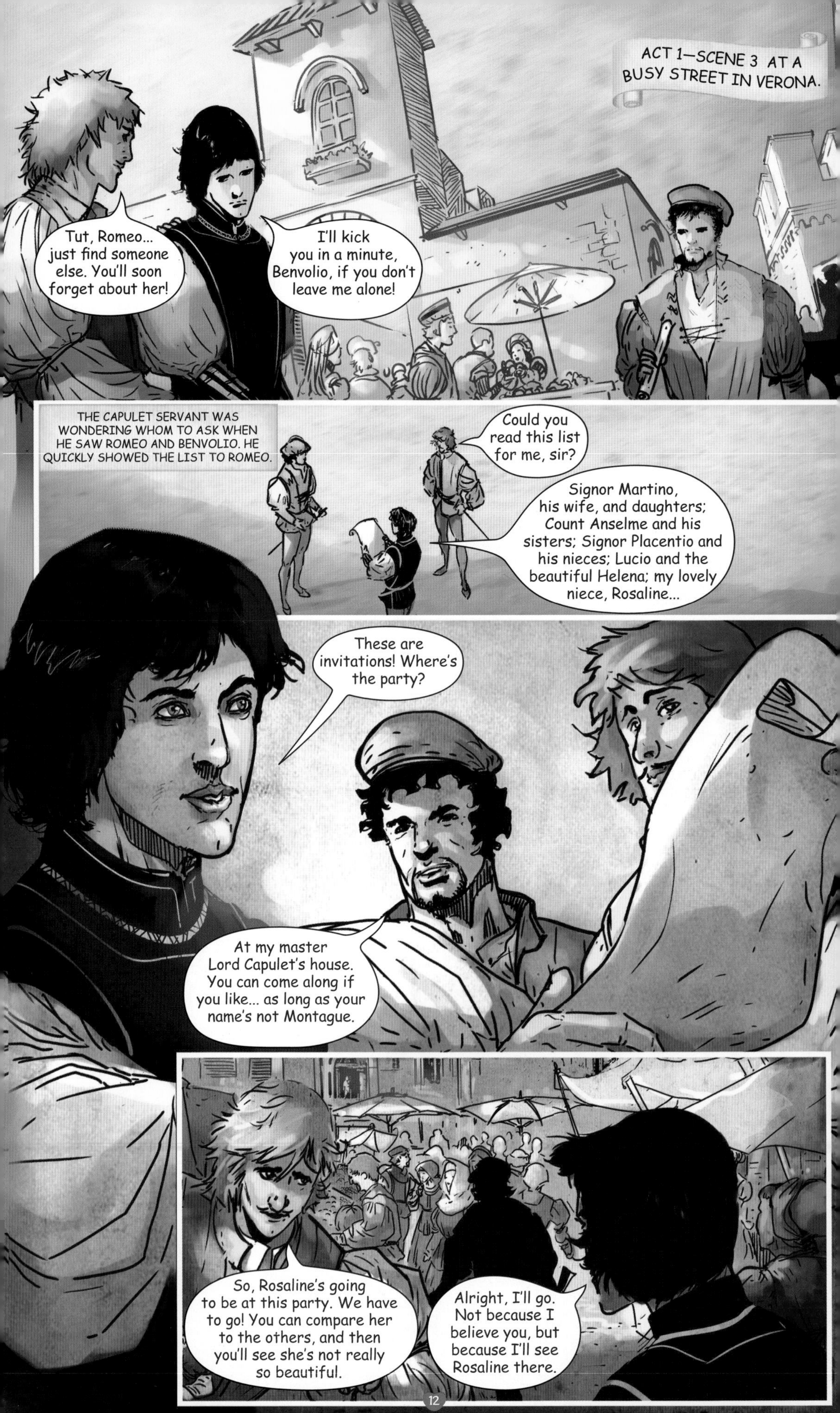

ACT 1—SCENE 3 AT A BUSY STREET IN VERONA.
Tut, Romeo... just find someone else. You'll soon forget about her!
I'll kick you in a minute, Benvolio, if you don't leave me alone!
THE CAPULET SERVANT WAS WONDERING WHOM TO ASK WHEN HE SAW ROMEO AND BENVOLIO. HE QUICKLY SHOWED THE LIST TO ROMEO.
Could you read this list for me, sir?
Signor Martino, his wife, and daughters; Count Anselme and his sisters; Signor Placentio and his nieces; Lucio and the beautiful Helena; my lovely niece, Rosaline...
These are invitations! Where's the party?
At my master Lord Capulet's house. You can come along if you like... as long as your name's not Montague.
So, Rosaline's going to be at this party. We have to go! You can compare her to the others, and then you'll see she's not really so beautiful.
Alright, I'll go. Not because I believe you, but because I'll see Rosaline there.

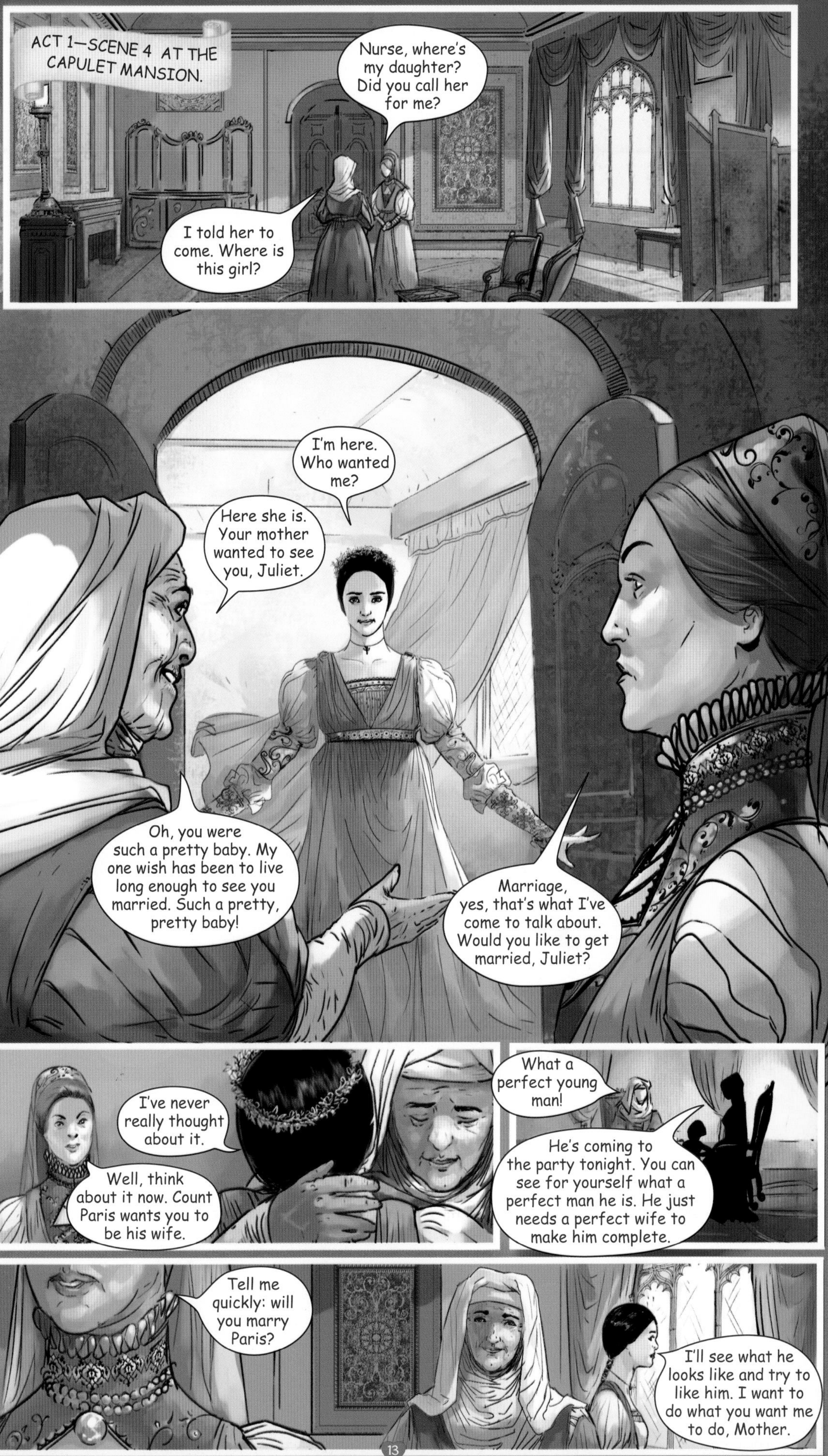
ACT 1—SCENE 4 AT THE CAPULET MANSION.
Nurse, where's my daughter? Did you call her for me?
I told her to come. Where is this girl?
I'm here. Who wanted me?
Here she is. Your mother wanted to see you, Juliet.
Oh, you were such a pretty baby. My one wish has been to live long enough to see you married. Such a pretty, pretty baby!
Marriage, yes, that's what I've come to talk about. Would you like to get married, Juliet?
I've never really thought about it.
Well, think about it now. Count Paris wants you to be his wife.
What a perfect young man!
He's coming to the party tonight. You can see for yourself what a perfect man he is. He just needs a perfect wife to make him complete.
Tell me quickly: will you marry Paris?
I'll see what he looks like and try to like him. I want to do what you want me to do, Mother.

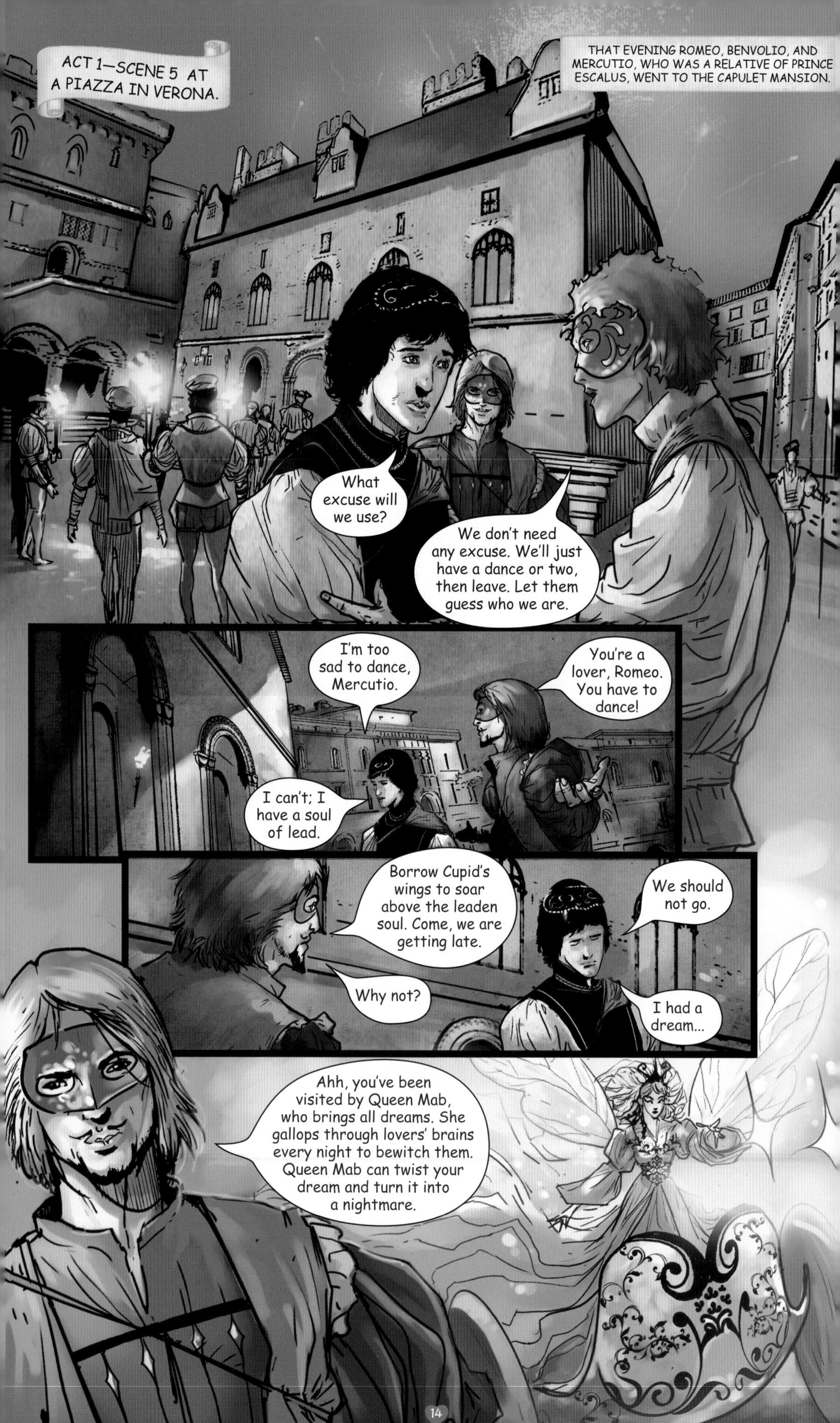
ACT 1—SCENE 5 AT A PIAZZA IN VERONA.
THAT EVENING ROMEO, BENVOLIO, AND MERCUTIO, WHO WAS A RELATIVE OF PRINCE ESCALUS, WENT TO THE CAPULET MANSION.
What excuse will we use?
We don't need any excuse. We'll just have a dance or two, then leave. Let them guess who we are.
I'm too sad to dance, Mercutio.
You're a lover, Romeo. You have to dance!
I can't; I have a soul of lead.
Borrow Cupid's wings to soar above the leaden soul. Come, we are getting late.
We should not go.
Why not?
I had a dream...
Ahh, you've been visited by Queen Mab, who brings all dreams. She gallops through lovers' brains every night to bewitch them. Queen Mab can twist your dream and turn it into a nightmare.

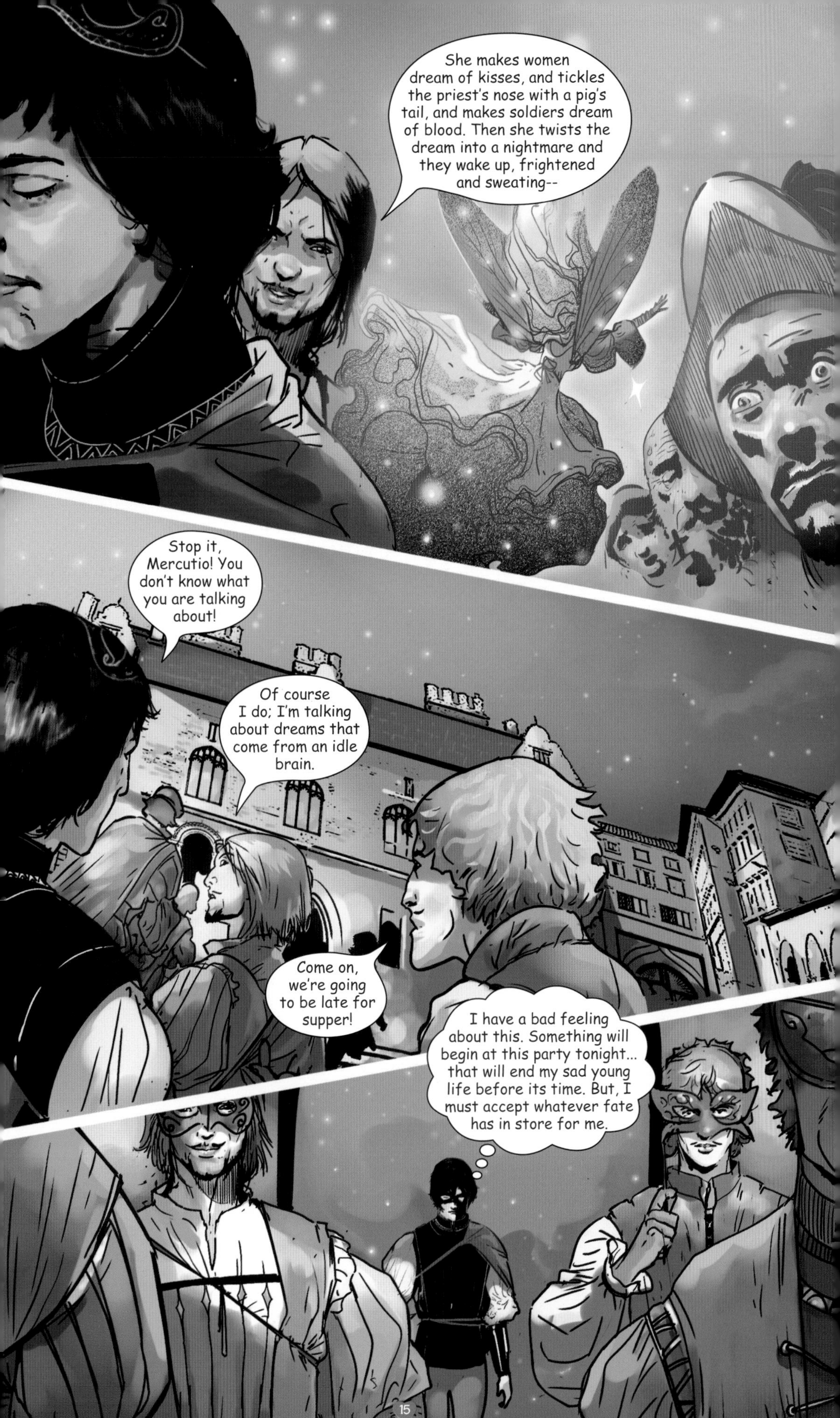

She makes women dream of kisses, and tickles the priest's nose with a pig's tail, and makes soldiers dream of blood. Then she twists the dream into a nightmare and they wake up, frightened and sweating--
Stop it, Mercutio! You don't know what you are talking about!
Of course I do; I'm talking about dreams that come from an idle brain.
Come on, we're going to be late for supper!
I have a bad feeling about this. Something will begin at this party tonight... that will end my sad young life before its time. But, I must accept whatever fate has in store for me.

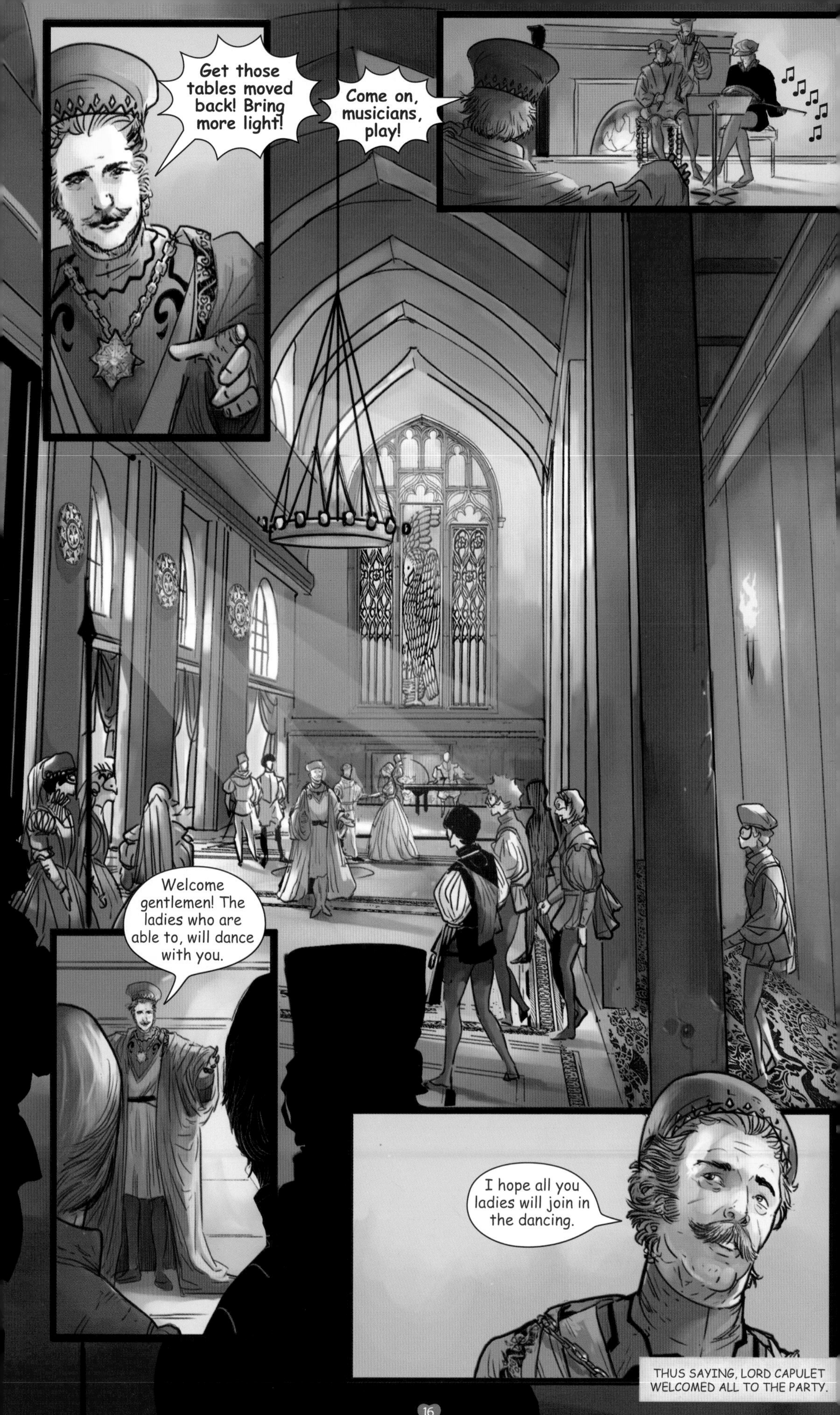
Get those tables moved back! Bring more light!
Come on, musicians, play!
Welcome gentlemen! The ladies who are able to, will dance with you.
I hope all you ladies will join in the dancing.
THUS SAYING, LORD CAPULET WELCOMED ALL TO THE PARTY.

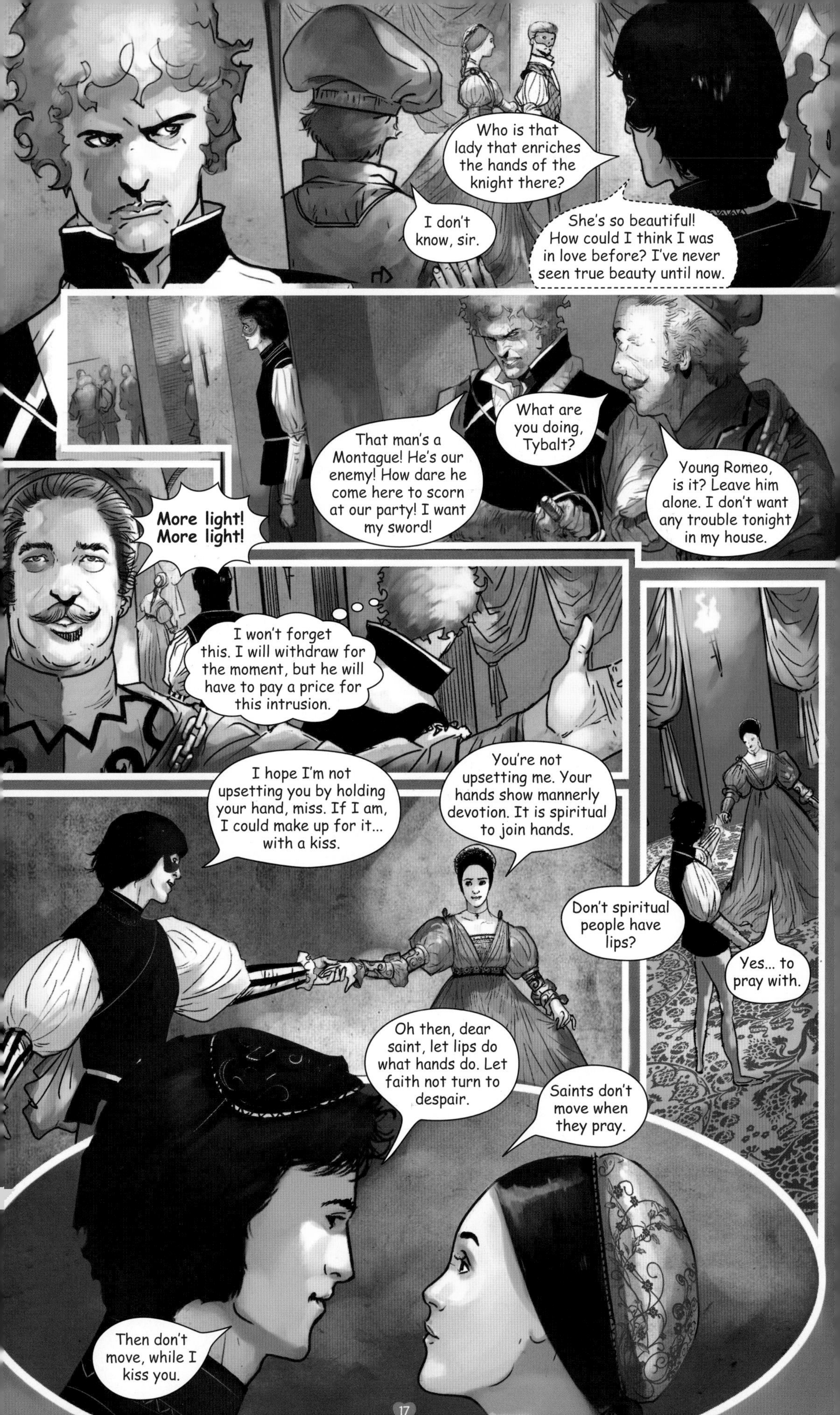
Who is that lady that enriches the hands of the knight there?
I don't know, sir.
She's so beautiful! How could I think I was in love before? I've never seen true beauty until now.
That man's a Montague! He's our enemy! How dare he come here to scorn at our party! I want my sword!
What are you doing, Tybalt?
Young Romeo, is it? Leave him alone. I don't want any trouble tonight in my house.
More light! More light!
I won't forget this. I will withdraw for the moment, but he will have to pay a price for this intrusion.
I hope I'm not upsetting you by holding your hand, miss. If I am, I could make up for it... with a kiss.
You're not upsetting me. Your hands show mannerly devotion. It is spiritual to join hands.
Don't spiritual people have lips?
Yes... to pray with.
Oh then, dear saint, let lips do what hands do. Let faith not turn to despair.
Saints don't move when they pray.
Then don't move, while I kiss you.

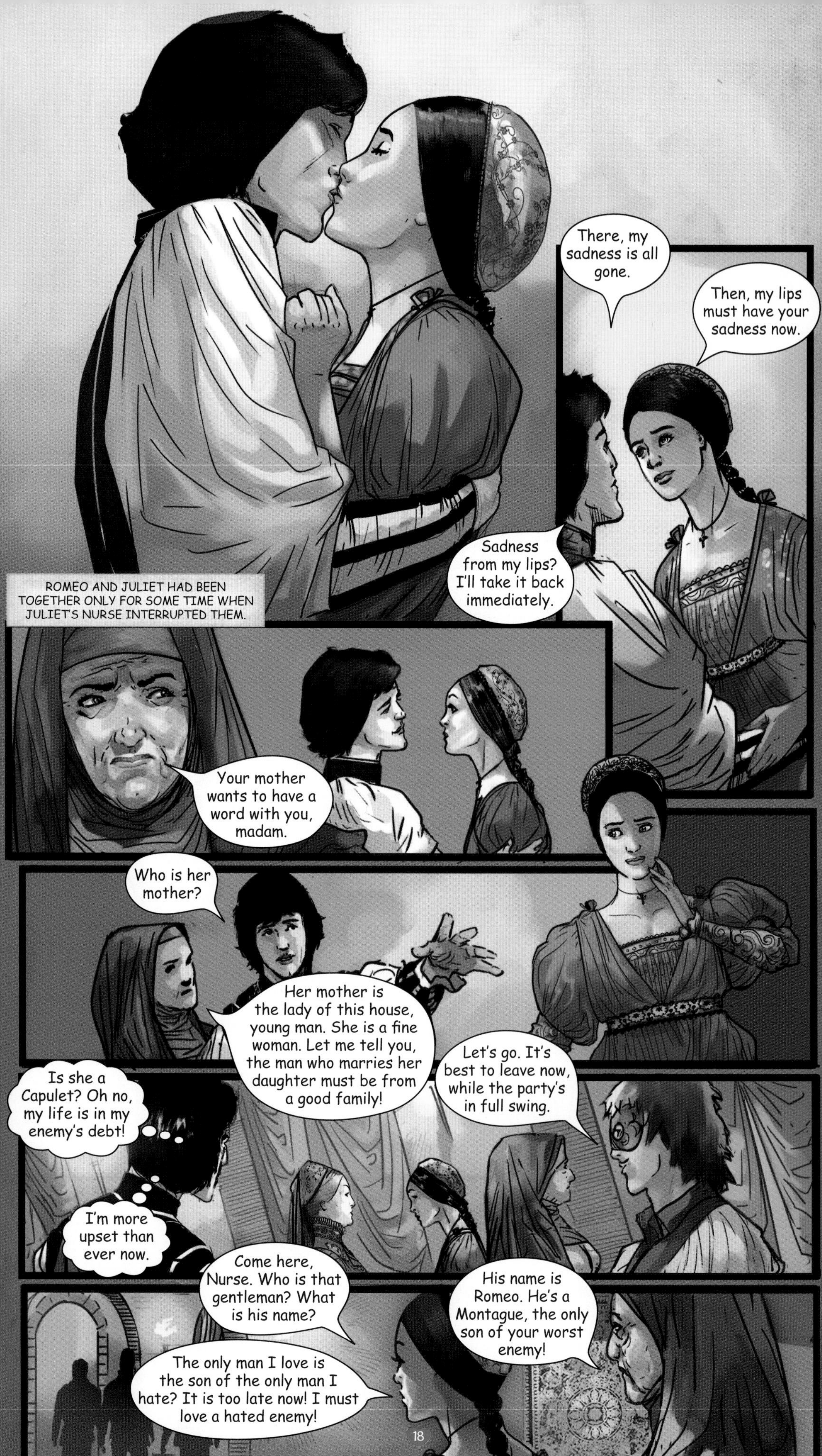
There, my sadness is all gone.
Then, my lips must have your sadness now.
Sadness from my lips? I'll take it back immediately.
ROMEO AND JULIET HAD BEEN TOGETHER ONLY FOR SOME TIME WHEN JULIET'S NURSE INTERRUPTED THEM.
Your mother wants to have a word with you, madam.
Who is her mother?
Her mother is the lady of this house, young man. She is a fine woman. Let me tell you, the man who marries her daughter must be from a good family!
Is she a Capulet? Oh no, my life is in my enemy's debt!
Let's go. It's best to leave now, while the party's in full swing.
I'm more upset than ever now.
Come here, Nurse. Who is that gentleman? What is his name?
His name is Romeo. He's a Montague, the only son of your worst enemy!
The only man I love is the son of the only man I hate? It is too late now! I must love a hated enemy!

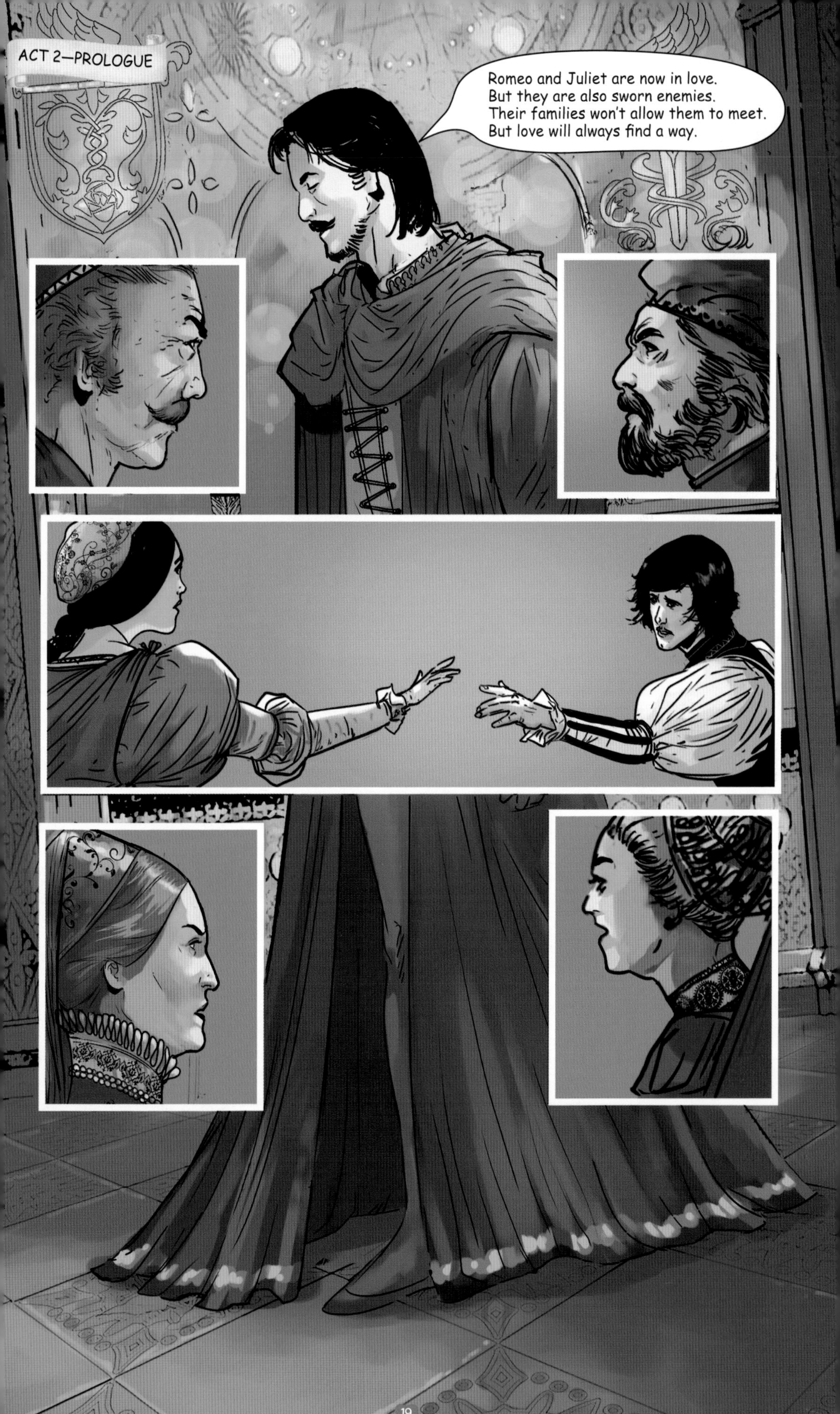
ACT 2—PROLOGUE
Romeo and Juliet are now in love. But they are also sworn enemies. Their families won't allow them to meet. But love will always find a way.

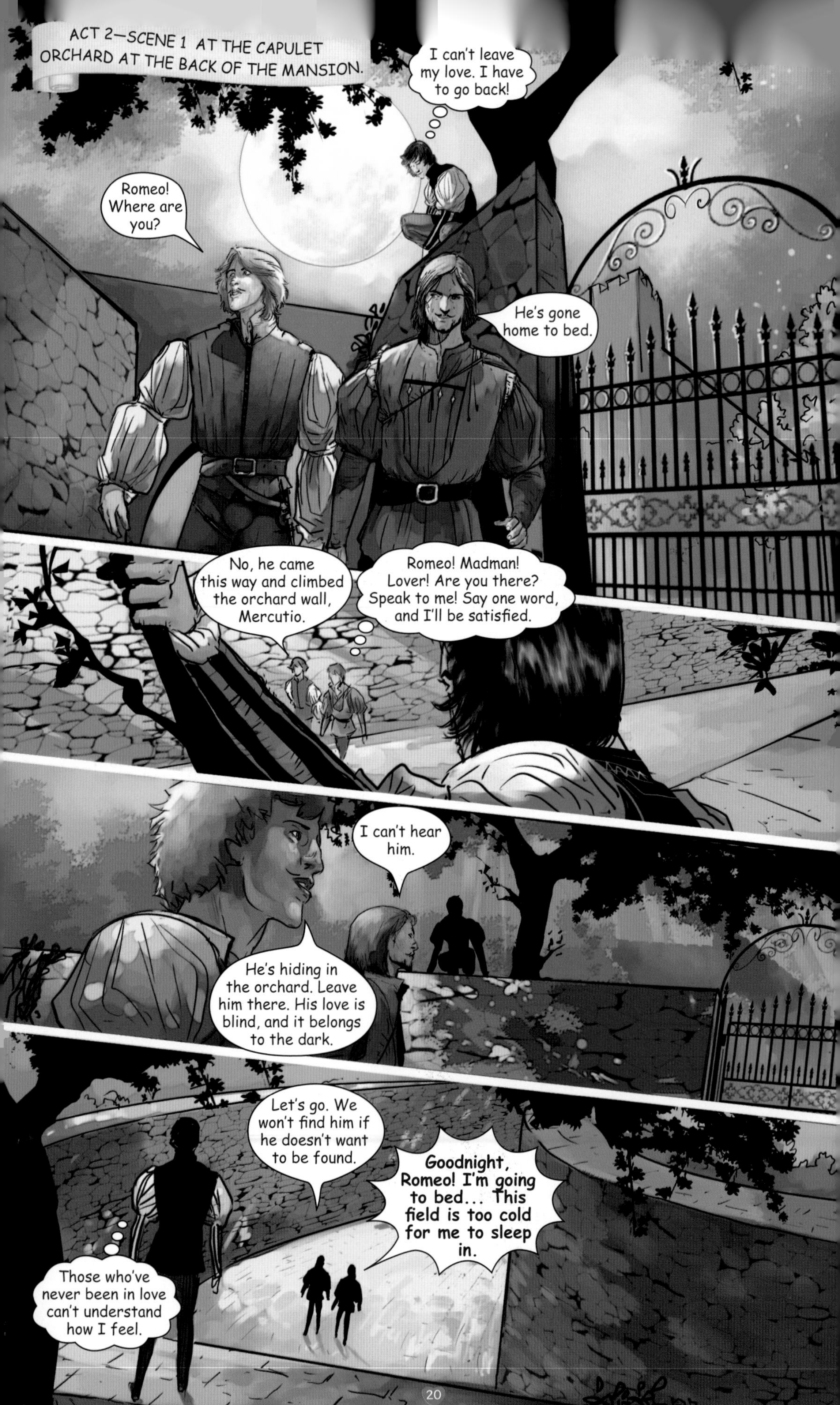
ACT 2—SCENE 1 AT THE CAPULET ORCHARD AT THE BACK OF THE MANSION.
I can't leave my love. I have to go back!
Romeo! Where are you?
He's gone home to bed.
No, he came this way and climbed the orchard wall, Mercutio.
Romeo! Madman! Lover! Are you there? Speak to me! Say one word, and I'll be satisfied.
I can't hear him.
He's hiding in the orchard. Leave him there. His love is blind, and it belongs to the dark.
Let's go. We won't find him if he doesn't want to be found.
Goodnight, Romeo! I'm going to bed... This field is too cold for me to sleep in.
Those who've never been in love can't understand how I feel.

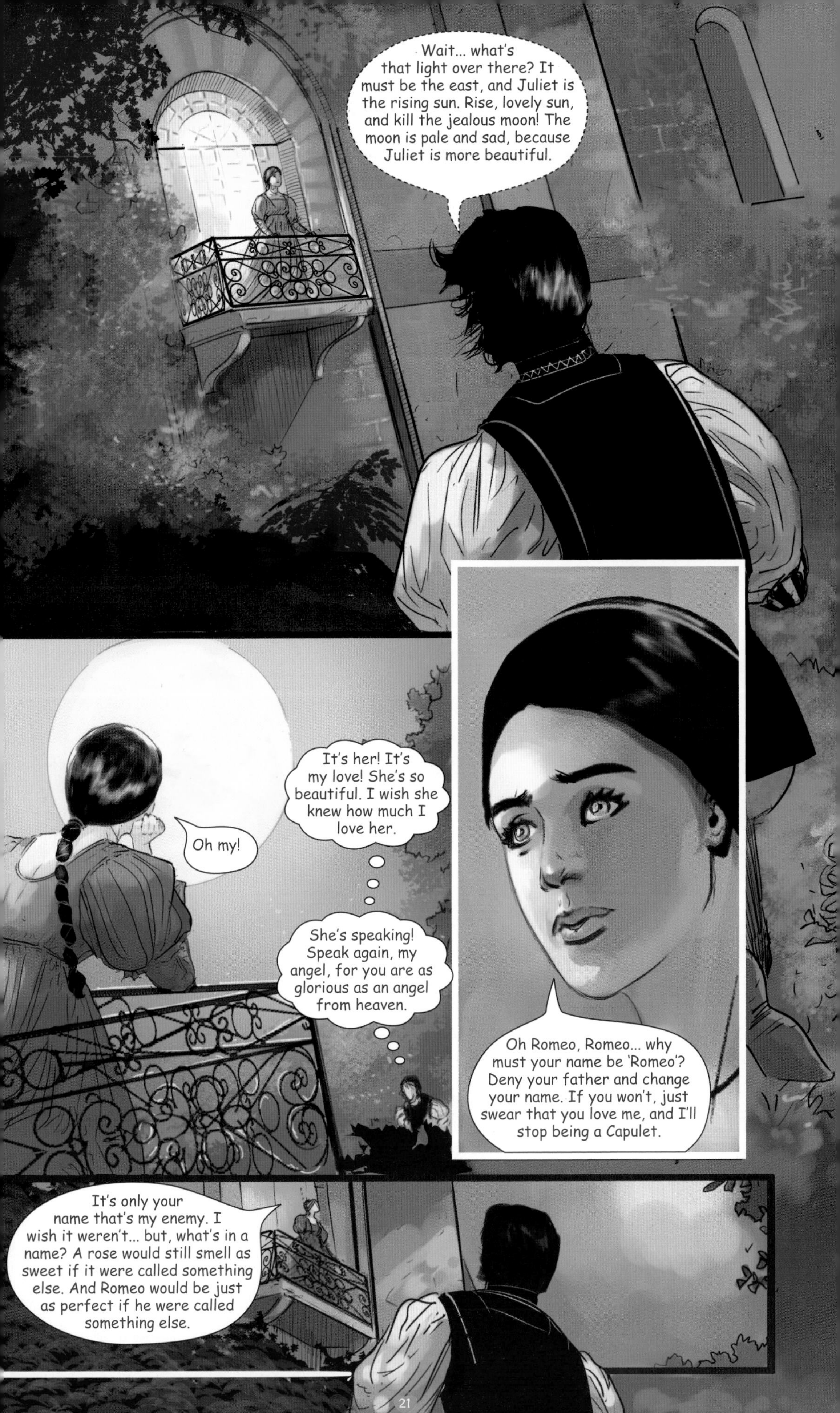
Wait... what's that light over there? It must be the east, and Juliet is the rising sun. Rise, lovely sun, and kill the jealous moon! The moon is pale and sad, because Juliet is more beautiful.
Oh my!
It's her! It's my love! She's so beautiful. I wish she knew how much I love her.
She's speaking! Speak again, my angel, for you are as glorious as an angel from heaven.
Oh Romeo, Romeo... why must your name be 'Romeo'? Deny your father and change your name. If you won't, just swear that you love me, and I'll stop being a Capulet.
It's only your name that's my enemy. I wish it weren't... but, what's in a name? A rose would still smell as sweet if it were called something else. And Romeo would be just as perfect if he were called something else.

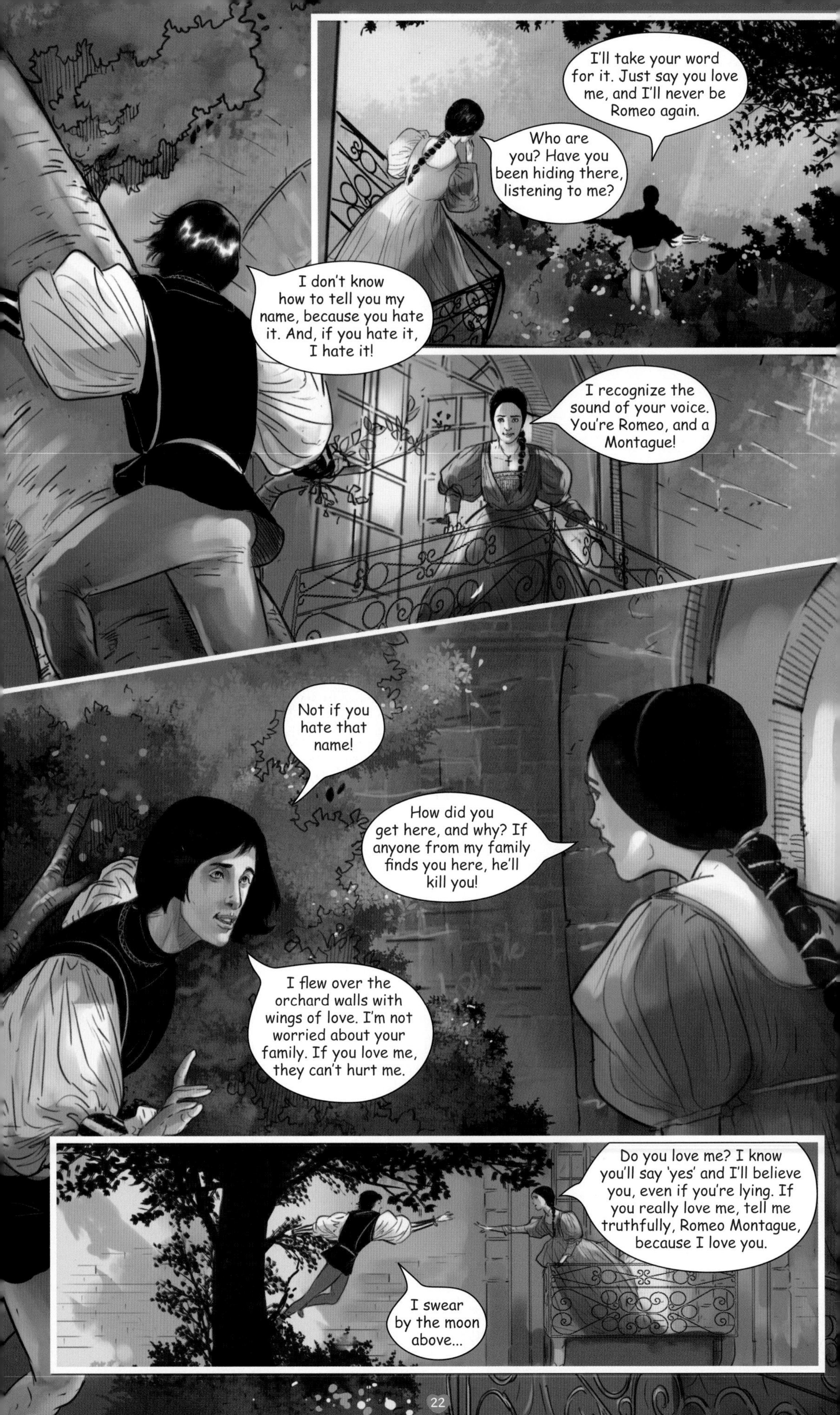
Who are you? Have you been hiding there, listening to me?
I'll take your word for it. Just say you love me, and I'll never be Romeo again.
I don't know how to tell you my name, because you hate it. And, if you hate it, I hate it!
I recognize the sound of your voice. You're Romeo, and a Montague!
Not if you hate that name!
How did you get here, and why? If anyone from my family finds you here, he'll kill you!
I flew over the orchard walls with wings of love. I'm not worried about your family. If you love me, they can't hurt me.
Do you love me? I know you'll say 'yes' and I'll believe you, even if you're lying. If you really love me, tell me truthfully, Romeo Montague, because I love you.
I swear by the moon above...

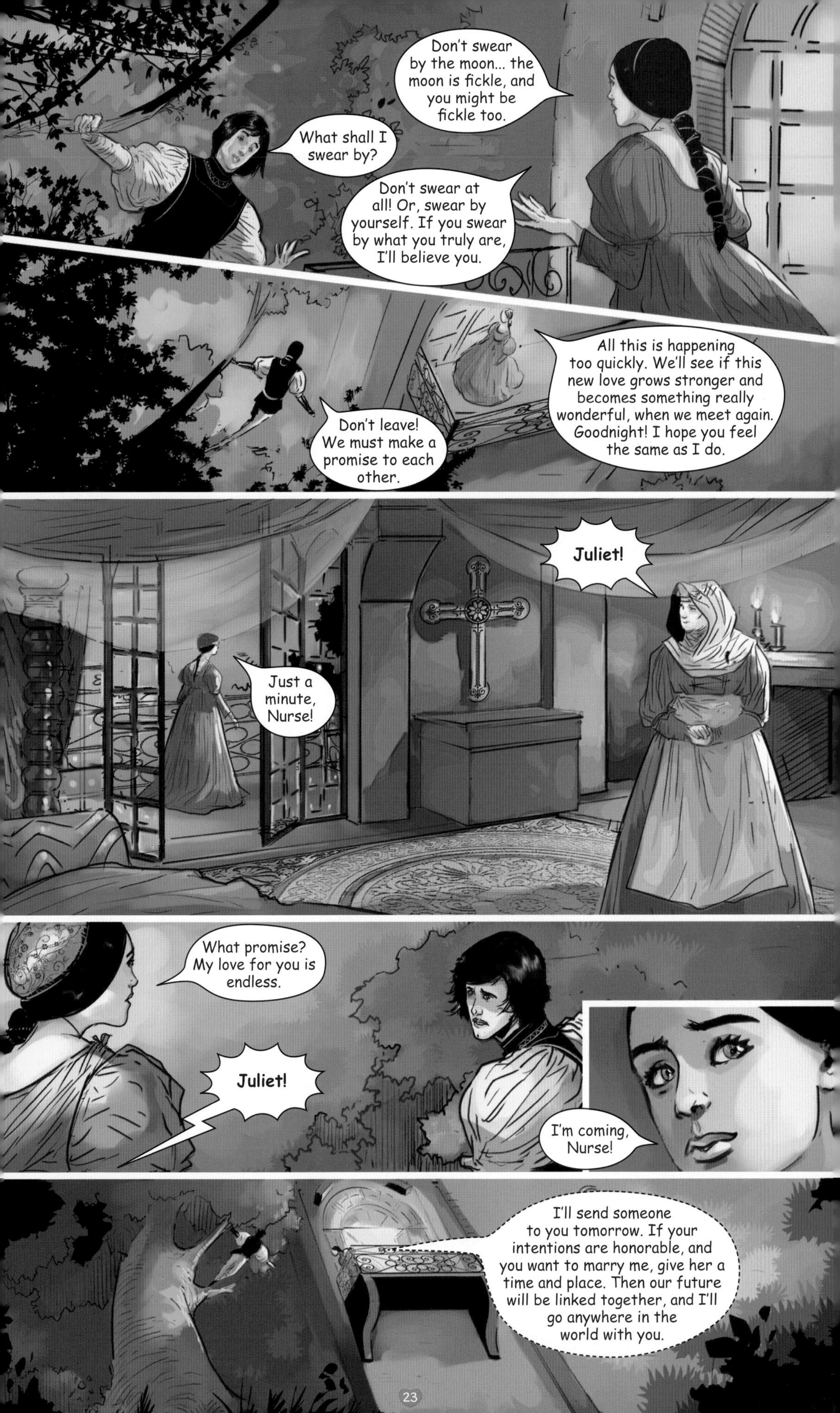
Don't swear by the moon... the moon is fickle, and you might be fickle too.
What shall I swear by?
Don't swear at all! Or, swear by yourself. If you swear by what you truly are, I'll believe you.
All this is happening too quickly. We'll see if this new love grows stronger and becomes something really wonderful, when we meet again. Goodnight! I hope you feel the same as I do.
Don't leave! We must make a promise to each other.
Juliet!
Just a minute, Nurse!
What promise? My love for you is endless.
Juliet!
I'm coming, Nurse!
I'll send someone to you tomorrow. If your intentions are honorable, and you want to marry me, give her a time and place. Then our future will be linked together, and I'll go anywhere in the world with you.

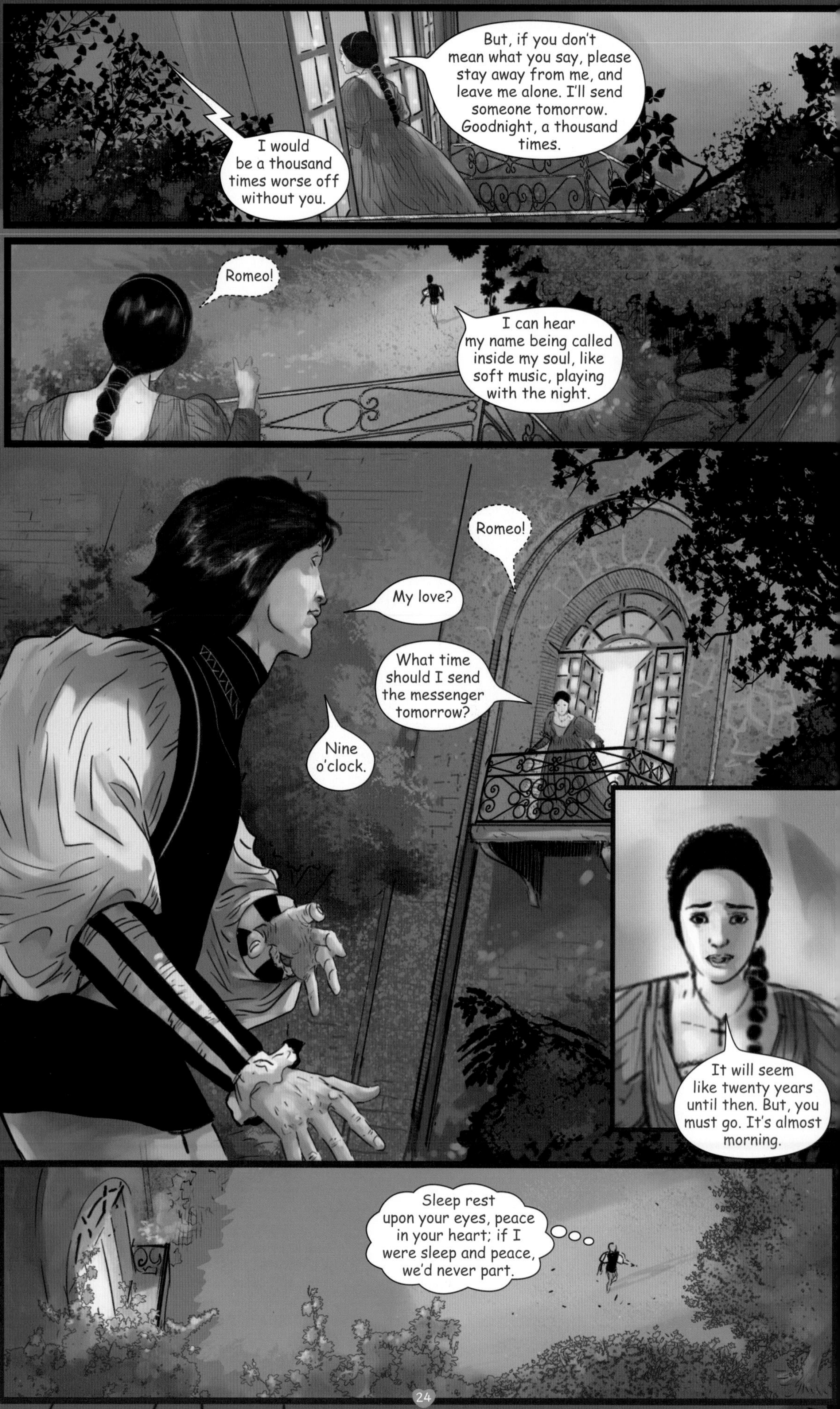
But, if you don't mean what you say, please stay away from me, and leave me alone. I'll send someone tomorrow. Goodnight, a thousand times.
I would be a thousand times worse off without you.
Romeo!
I can hear my name being called inside my soul, like soft music, playing with the night.
Romeo!
My love?
What time should I send the messenger tomorrow?
Nine o'clock.
It will seem like twenty years until then. But, you must go. It's almost morning.
Sleep rest upon your eyes, peace in your heart; if I were sleep and peace, we'd never part.

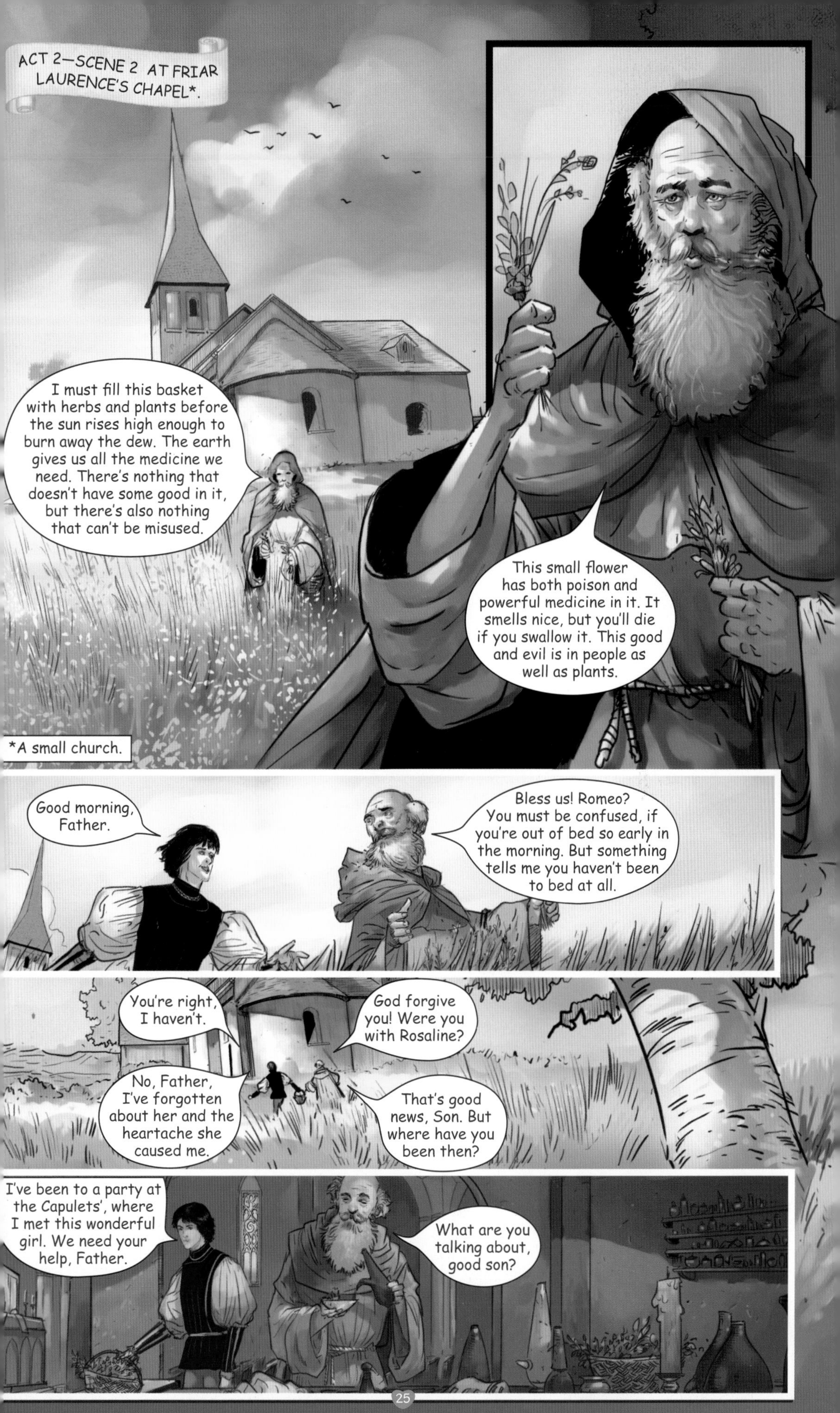
ACT 2—SCENE 2 AT FRIAR LAURENCE'S CHAPEL*.
I must fill this basket with herbs and plants before the sun rises high enough to burn away the dew. The earth gives us all the medicine we need. There's nothing that doesn't have some good in it, but there's also nothing that can't be misused.
This small flower has both poison and powerful medicine in it. It smells nice, but you'll die if you swallow it. This good and evil is in people as well as plants.
*A small church.
Good morning, Father.
Bless us! Romeo? You must be confused, if you're out of bed so early in the morning. But something tells me you haven't been to bed at all.
You're right, I haven't.
God forgive you! Were you with Rosaline?
No, Father, I've forgotten about her and the heartache she caused me.
That's good news, Son. But where have you been then?
I've been to a party at the Capulets', where I met this wonderful girl. We need your help, Father.
What are you talking about, good son?

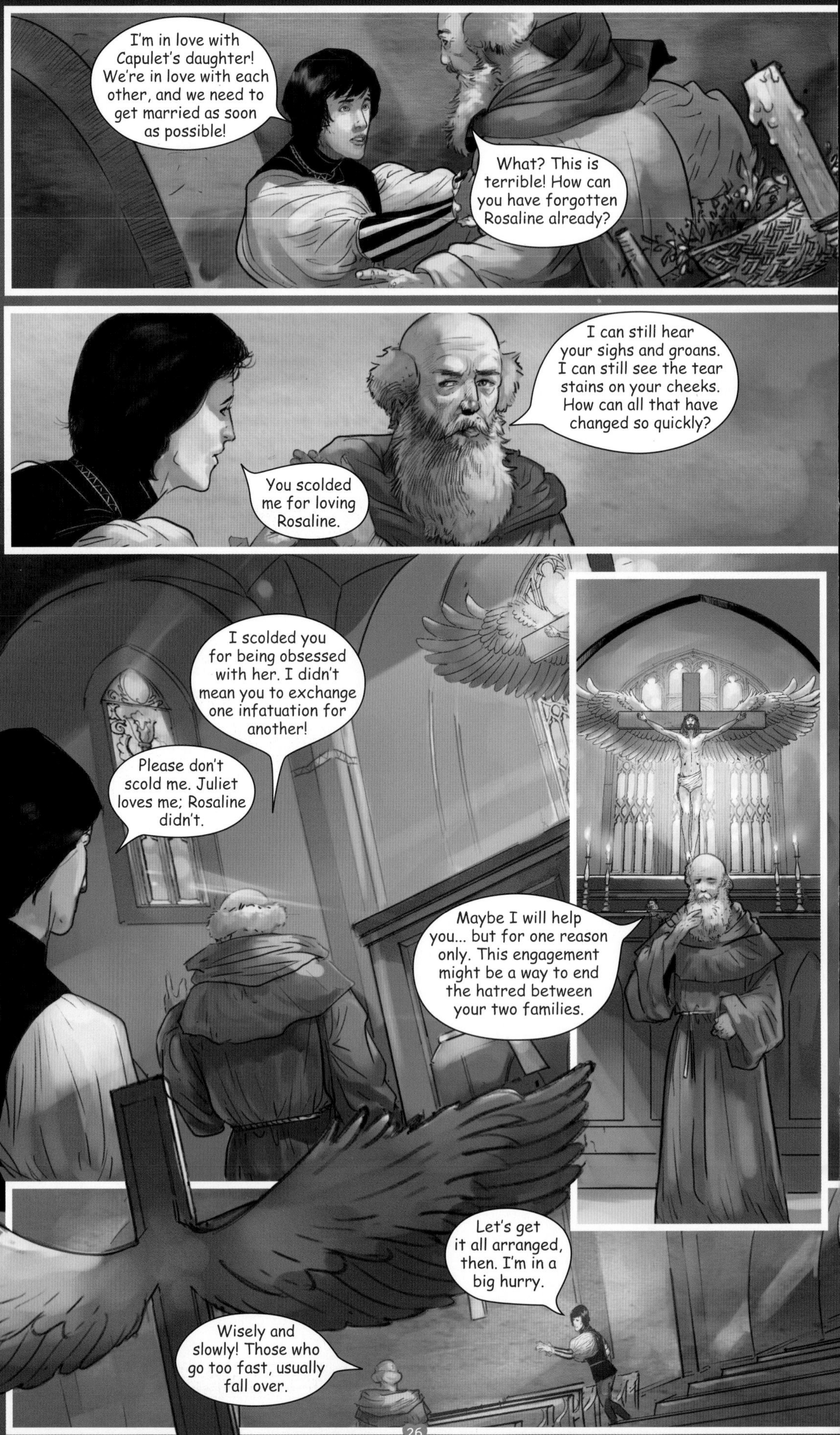
I'm in love with Capulet's daughter! We're in love with each other, and we need to get married as soon as possible!
What? This is terrible! How can you have forgotten Rosaline already?
I can still hear your sighs and groans. I can still see the tear stains on your cheeks. How can all that have changed so quickly?
You scolded me for loving Rosaline.
I scolded you for being obsessed with her. I didn't mean you to exchange one infatuation for another!
Please don't scold me. Juliet loves me; Rosaline didn't.
Maybe I will help you... but for one reason only. This engagement might be a way to end the hatred between your two families.
Let's get it all arranged, then. I'm in a big hurry.
Wisely and slowly! Those who go too fast, usually fall over.

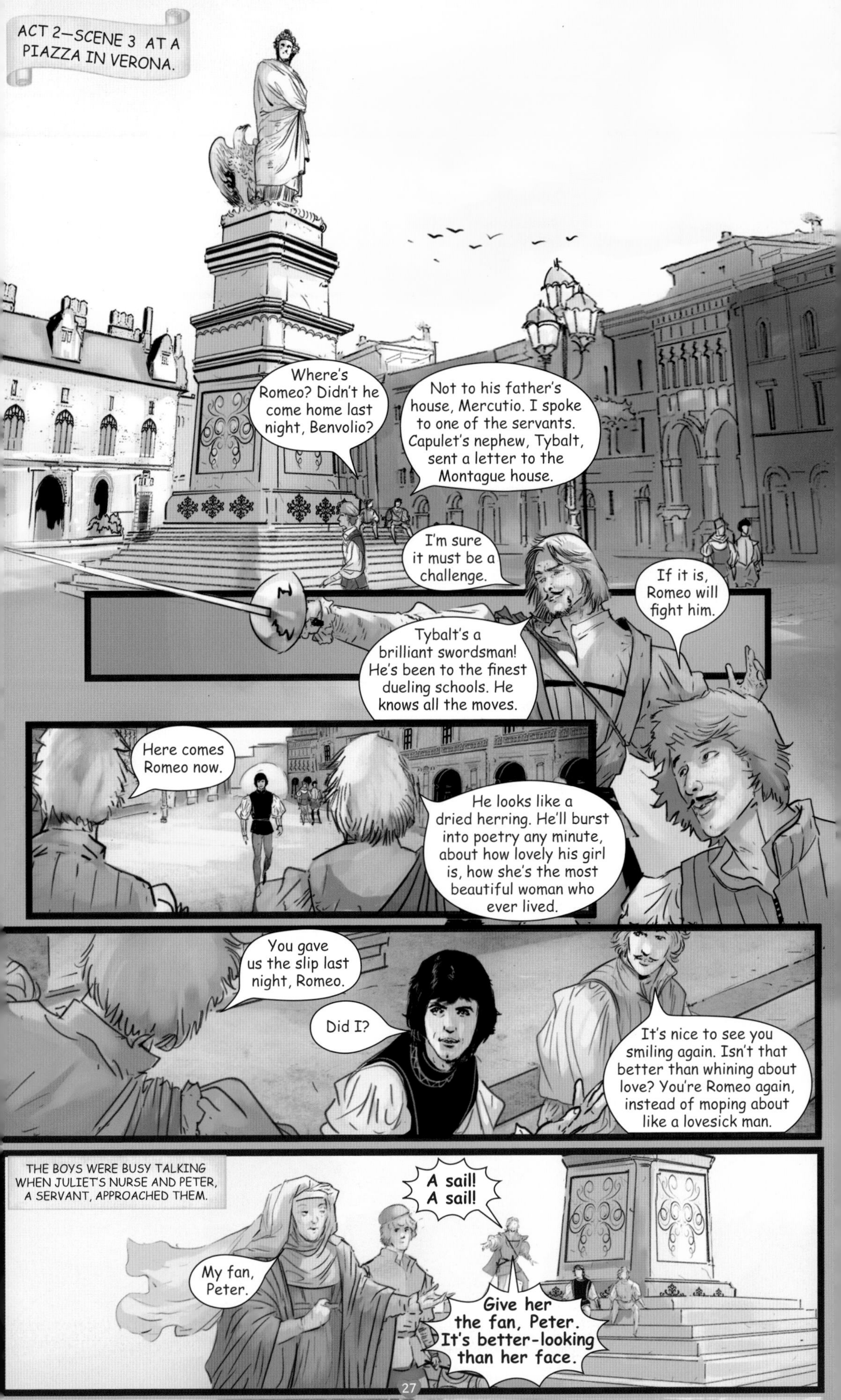
ACT 2—SCENE 3 AT A PIAZZA IN VERONA.
Where's Romeo? Didn't he come home last night, Benvolio?
Not to his father's house, Mercutio. I spoke to one of the servants. Capulet's nephew, Tybalt, sent a letter to the Montague house.
I'm sure it must be a challenge.
If it is, Romeo will fight him.
Tybalt's a brilliant swordsman! He's been to the finest dueling schools. He knows all the moves.
Here comes Romeo now.
He looks like a dried herring. He'll burst into poetry any minute, about how lovely his girl is, how she's the most beautiful woman who ever lived.
You gave us the slip last night, Romeo.
Did I?
It's nice to see you smiling again. Isn't that better than whining about love? You're Romeo again, instead of moping about like a lovesick man.
THE BOYS WERE BUSY TALKING WHEN JULIET'S NURSE AND PETER, A SERVANT, APPROACHED THEM.
A sail! A sail!
My fan, Peter.
Give her the fan, Peter. It's better-looking than her face.

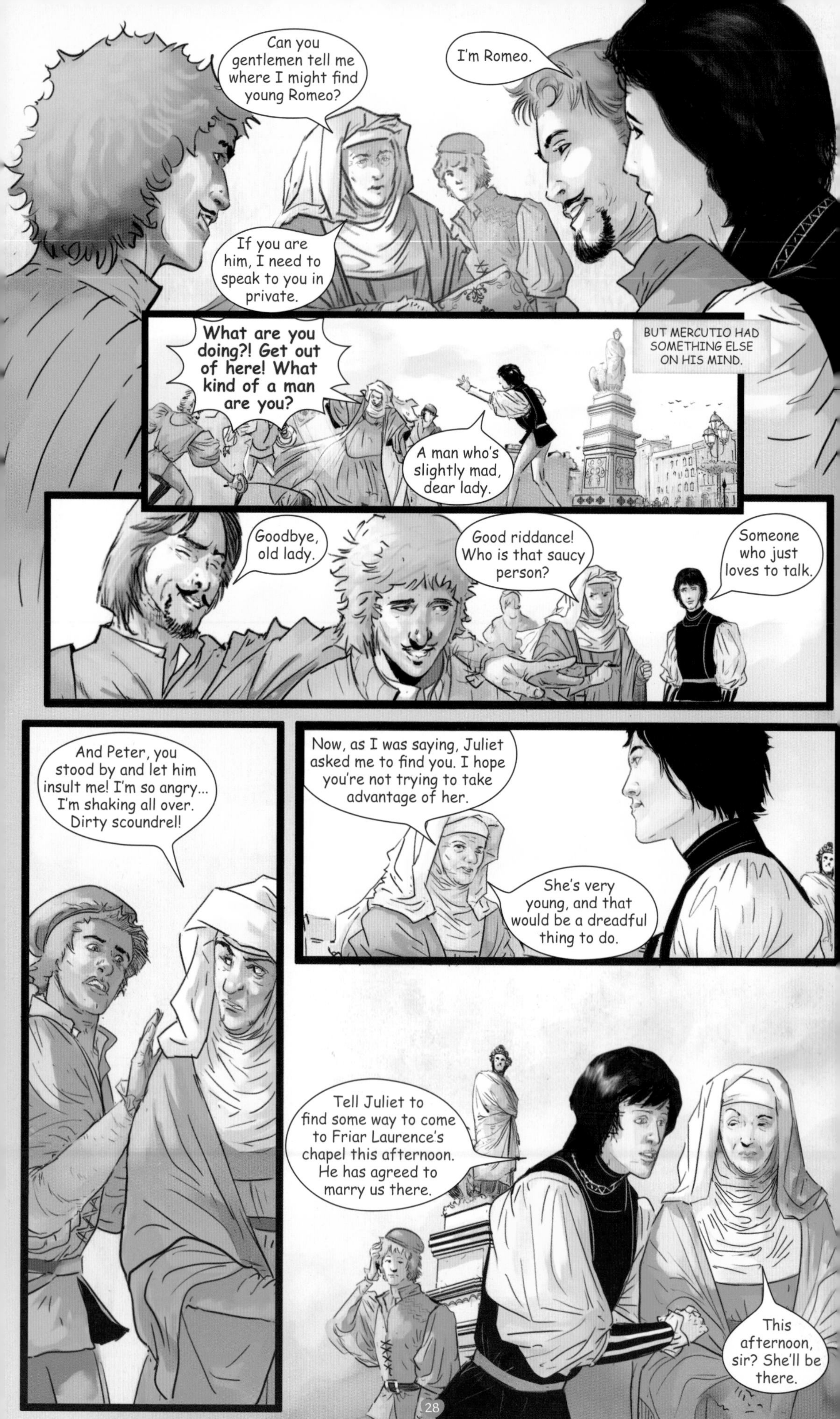
Can you gentlemen tell me where I might find young Romeo?
I'm Romeo.
If you are him, I need to speak to you in private.
BUT MERCUTIO HAD SOMETHING ELSE ON HIS MIND.
What are you doing?! Get out of here! What kind of a man are you?
A man who's slightly mad, dear lady.
Goodbye, old lady.
Good riddance! Who is that saucy person?
Someone who just loves to talk.
And Peter, you stood by and let him insult me! I'm so angry... I'm shaking all over. Dirty scoundrel!
Now, as I was saying, Juliet asked me to find you. I hope you're not trying to take advantage of her.
She's very young, and that would be a dreadful thing to do.
Tell Juliet to find some way to come to Friar Laurence's chapel this afternoon. He has agreed to marry us there.
This afternoon, sir? She'll be there.

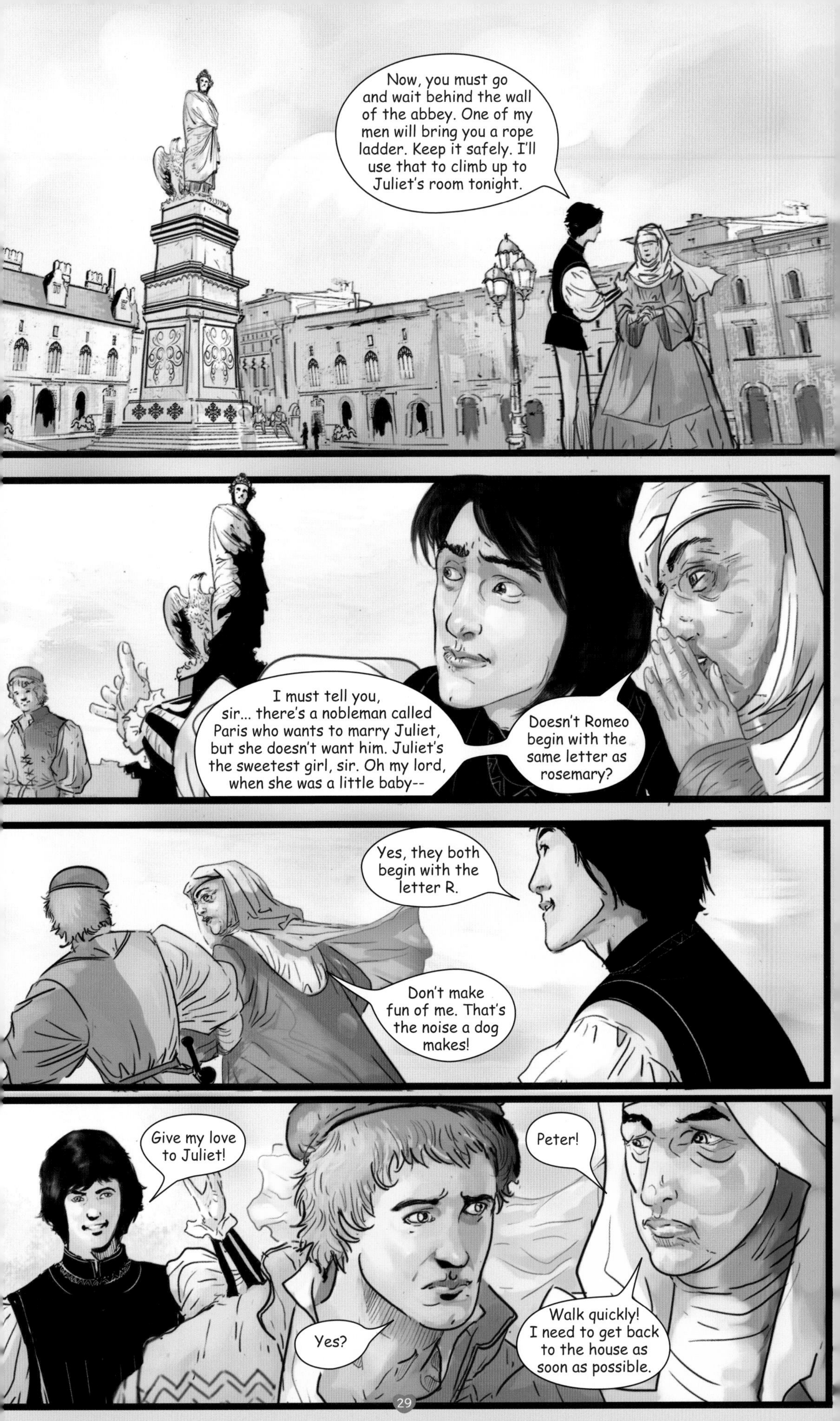
Now, you must go and wait behind the wall of the abbey. One of my men will bring you a rope ladder. Keep it safely. I'll use that to climb up to Juliet's room tonight.
I must tell you, sir... there's a nobleman called Paris who wants to marry Juliet, but she doesn't want him. Juliet's the sweetest girl, sir. Oh my lord, when she was a little baby--
Doesn't Romeo begin with the same letter as rosemary?
Yes, they both begin with the letter R.
Don't make fun of me. That's the noise a dog makes!
Give my love to Juliet!
Peter!
Yes?
Walk quickly! I need to get back to the house as soon as possible.

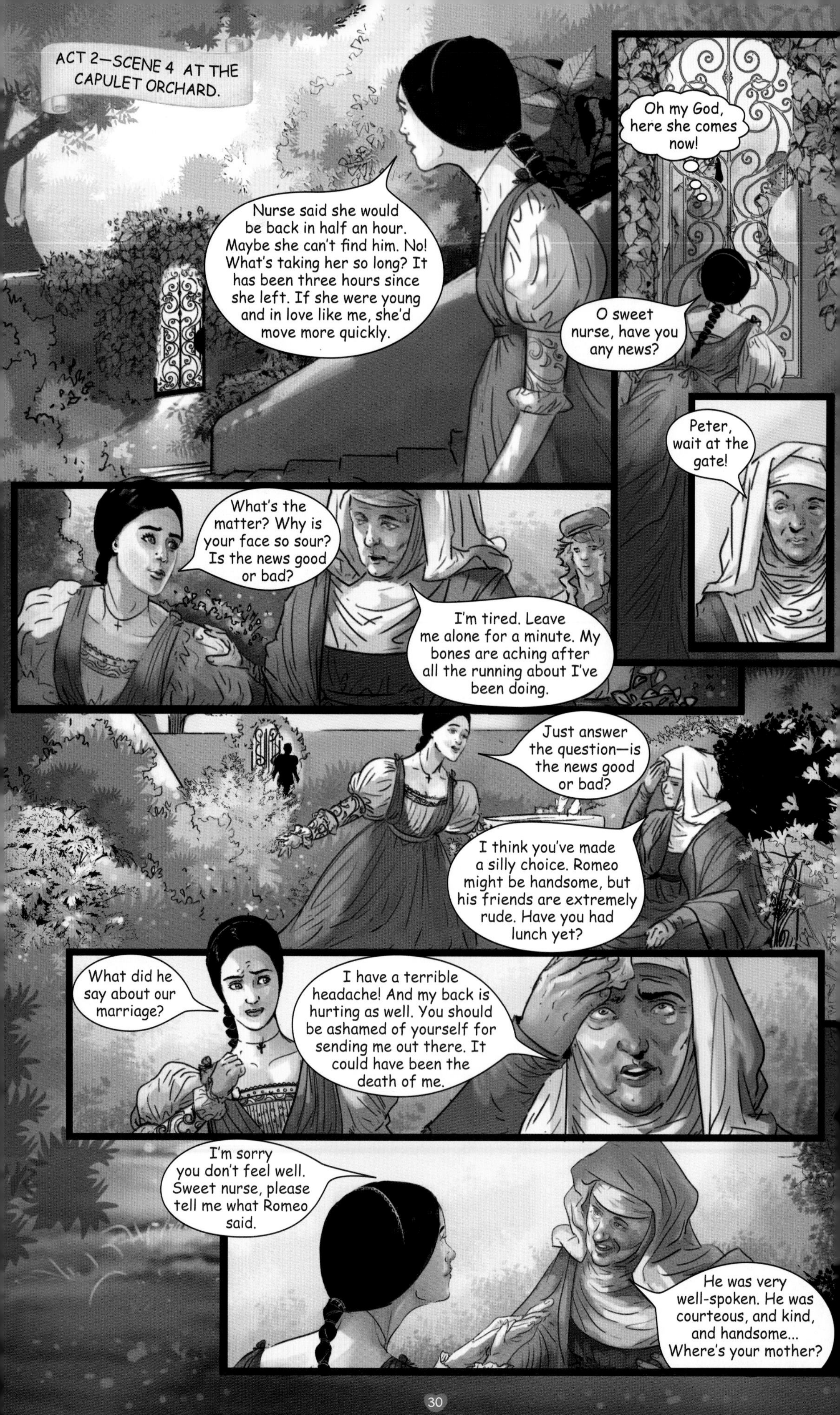
ACT 2—SCENE 4 AT THE CAPULET ORCHARD.
Nurse said she would be back in half an hour. Maybe she can't find him. No! What's taking her so long? It has been three hours since she left. If she were young and in love like me, she'd move more quickly.
Oh my God, here she comes now!
O sweet nurse, have you any news?
Peter, wait at the gate!
What's the matter? Why is your face so sour? Is the news good or bad?
I'm tired. Leave me alone for a minute. My bones are aching after all the running about I've been doing.
Just answer the question—is the news good or bad?
I think you've made a silly choice. Romeo might be handsome, but his friends are extremely rude. Have you had lunch yet?
What did he say about our marriage?
I have a terrible headache! And my back is hurting as well. You should be ashamed of yourself for sending me out there. It could have been the death of me.
I'm sorry you don't feel well. Sweet nurse, please tell me what Romeo said.
He was very well-spoken. He was courteous, and kind, and handsome... Where's your mother?

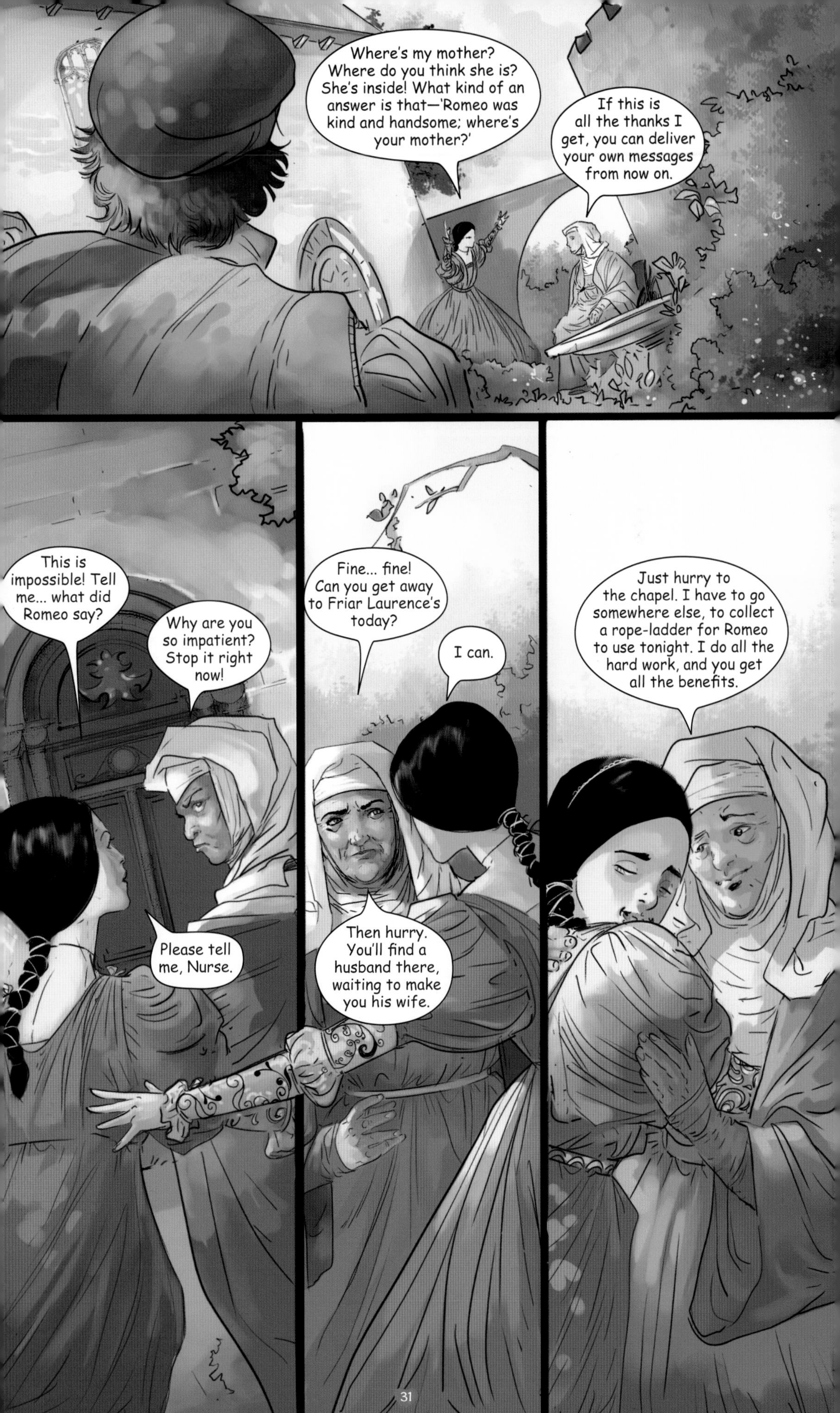

Where's my mother? Where do you think she is? She's inside! What kind of an answer is that—'Romeo was kind and handsome; where's your mother?'
If this is all the thanks I get, you can deliver your own messages from now on.
This is impossible! Tell me... what did Romeo say?
Why are you so impatient? Stop it right now!
Please tell me, Nurse.
Fine... fine! Can you get away to Friar Laurence's today?
I can.
Then hurry. You'll find a husband there, waiting to make you his wife.
Just hurry to the chapel. I have to go somewhere else, to collect a rope-ladder for Romeo to use tonight. I do all the hard work, and you get all the benefits.

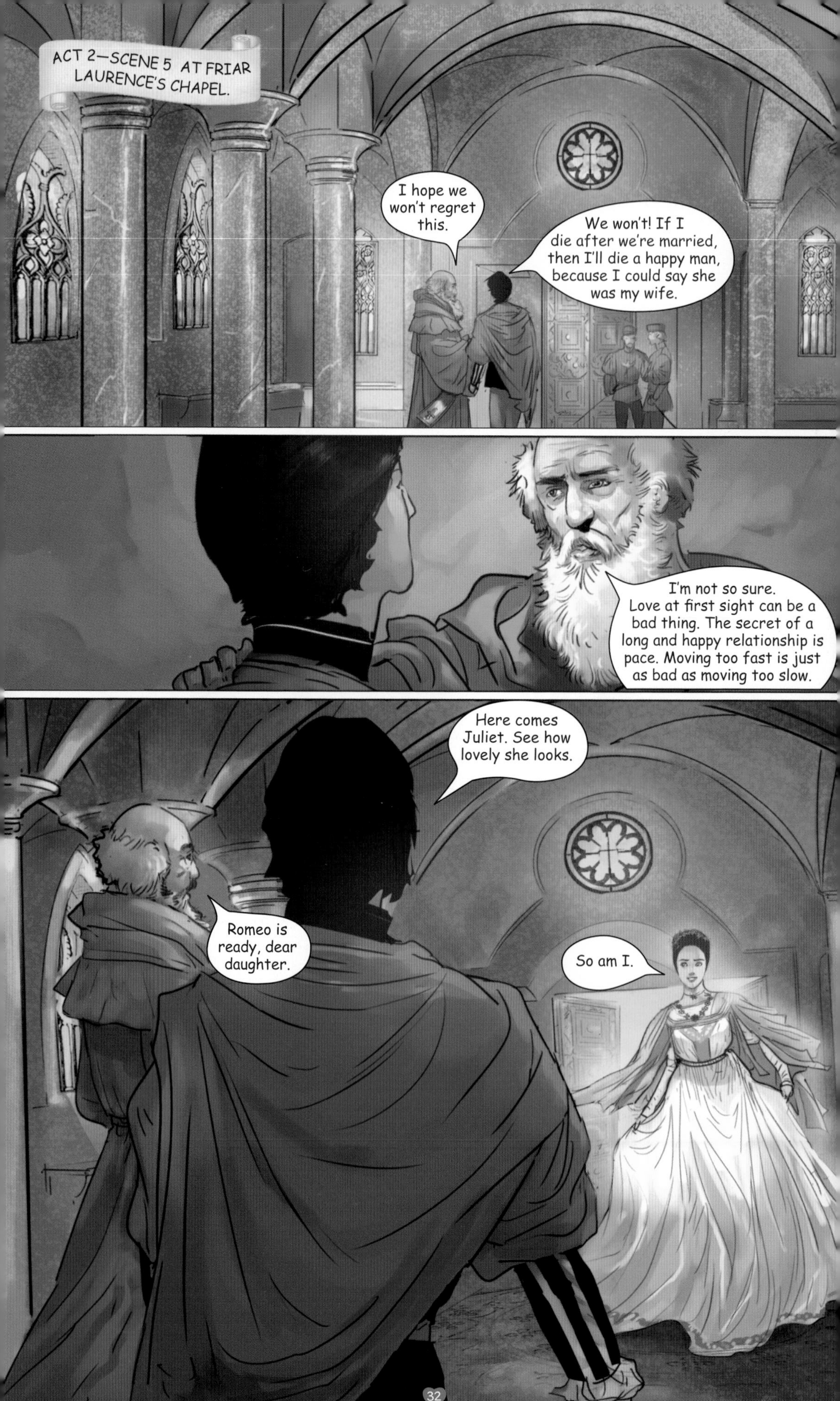
ACT 2—SCENE 5 AT FRIAR LAURENCE'S CHAPEL.
I hope we won't regret this.
We won't! If I die after we're married, then I'll die a happy man, because I could say she was my wife.
I'm not so sure. Love at first sight can be a bad thing. The secret of a long and happy relationship is pace. Moving too fast is just as bad as moving too slow.
Here comes Juliet. See how lovely she looks.
Romeo is ready, dear daughter.
So am I.

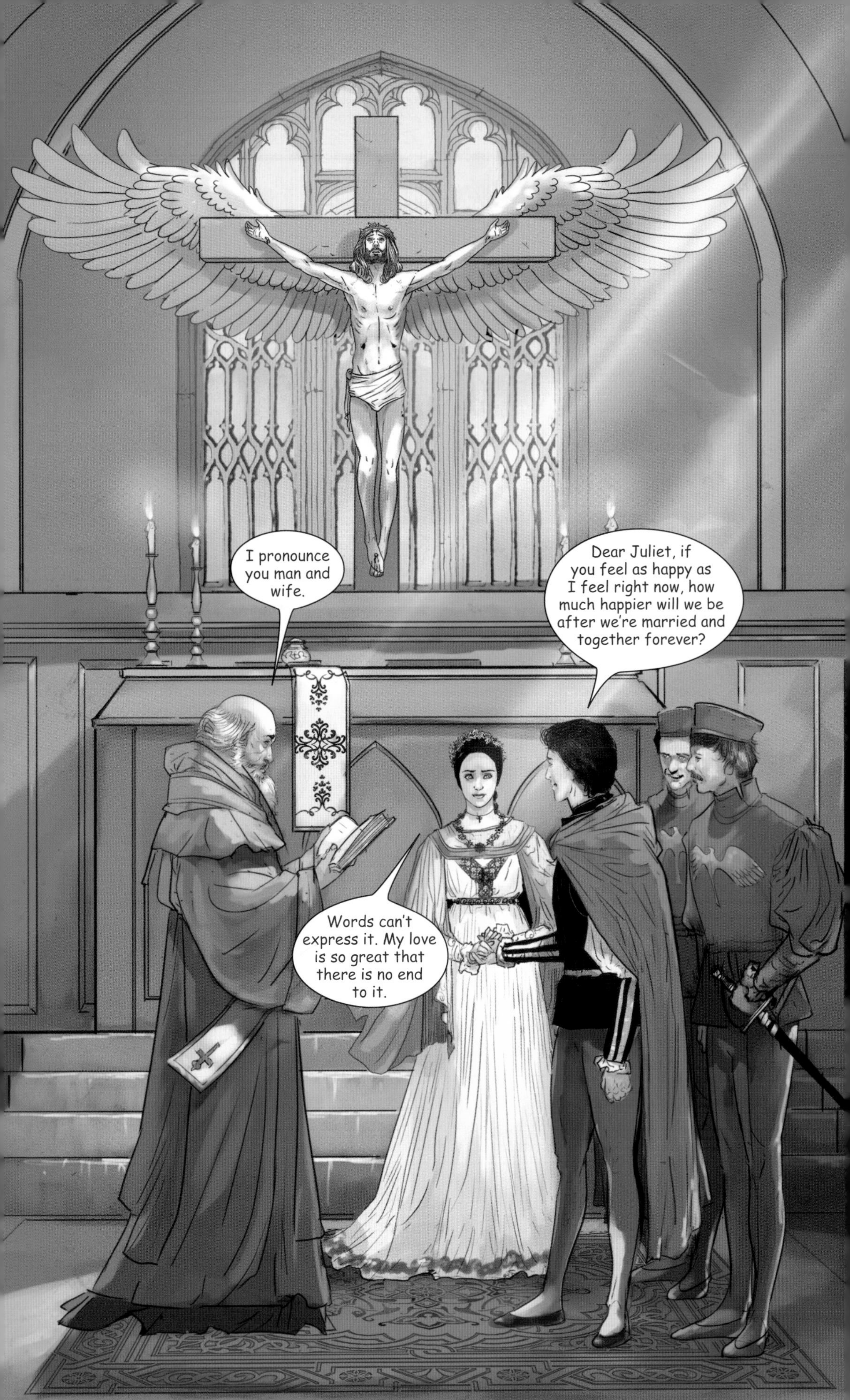
I pronounce you man and wife.
Dear Juliet, if you feel as happy as I feel right now, how much happier will we be after we're married and together forever?
Words can't express it. My love is so great that there is no end to it.

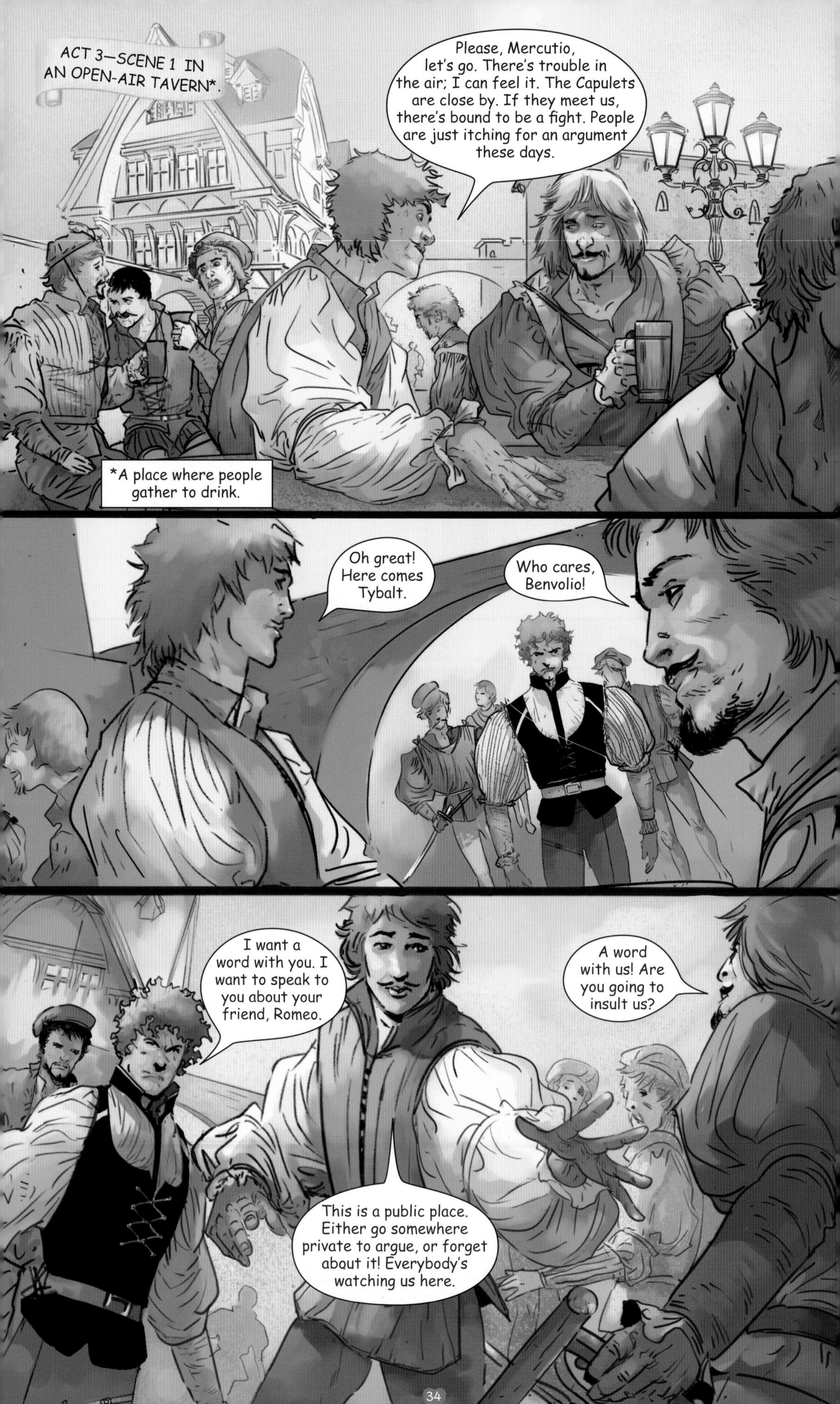
ACT 3—SCENE 1 IN AN OPEN-AIR TAVERN*.
Please, Mercutio, let's go. There's trouble in the air; I can feel it. The Capulets are close by. If they meet us, there's bound to be a fight. People are just itching for an argument these days.
*A place where people gather to drink.
Oh great! Here comes Tybalt.
Who cares, Benvolio!
I want a word with you. I want to speak to you about your friend, Romeo.
A word with us! Are you going to insult us?
This is a public place. Either go somewhere private to argue, or forget about it! Everybody's watching us here.

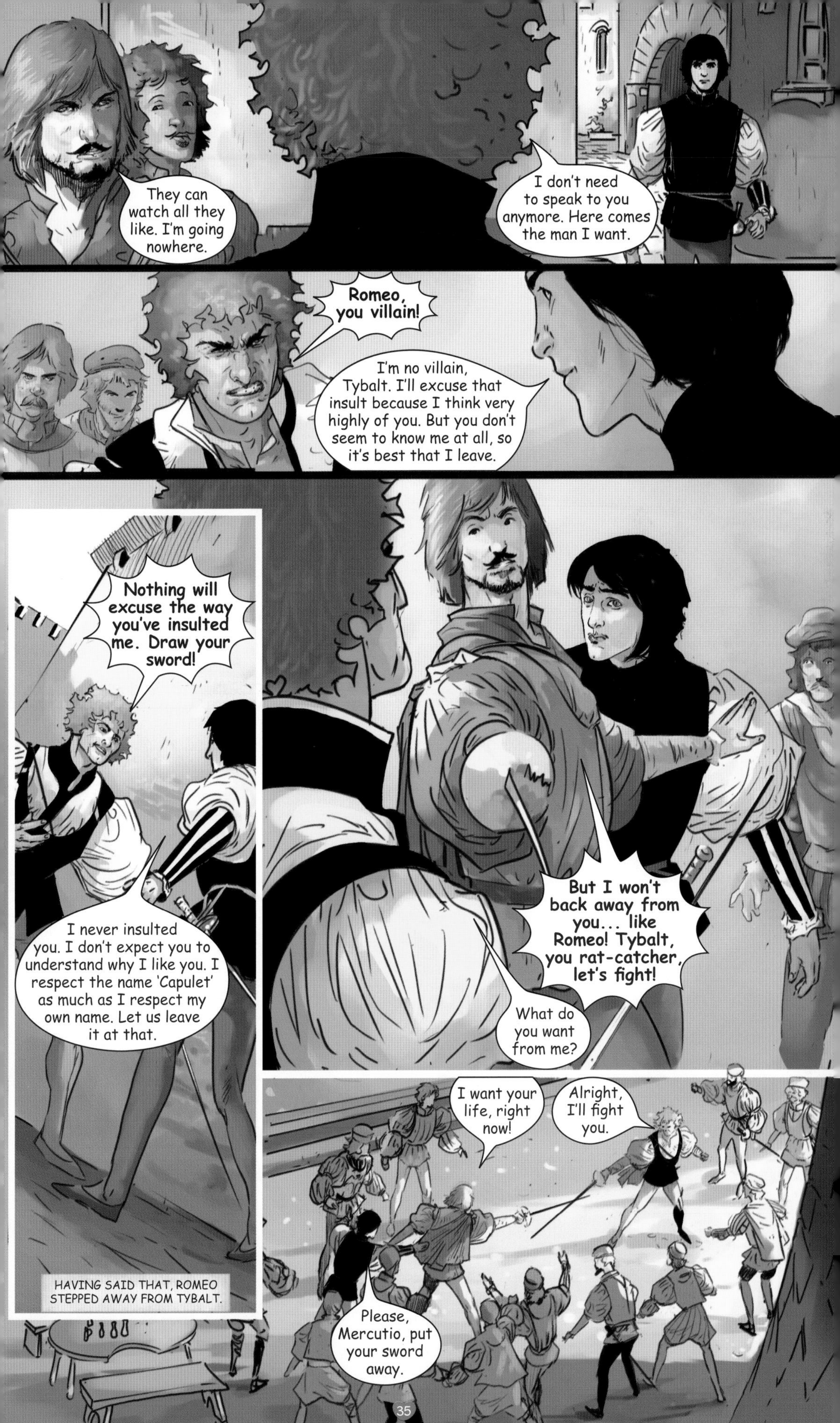
They can watch all they like. I'm going nowhere.
I don't need to speak to you anymore. Here comes the man I want.
Romeo, you villain!
I'm no villain, Tybalt. I'll excuse that insult because I think very highly of you. But you don't seem to know me at all, so it's best that I leave.
Nothing will excuse the way you've insulted me. Draw your sword!
I never insulted you. I don't expect you to understand why I like you. I respect the name 'Capulet' as much as I respect my own name. Let us leave it at that.
HAVING SAID THAT, ROMEO STEPPED AWAY FROM TYBALT.
But I won't back away from you... like Romeo! Tybalt, you rat-catcher, let's fight!
What do you want from me?
I want your life, right now!
Alright, I'll fight you.
Please, Mercutio, put your sword away.

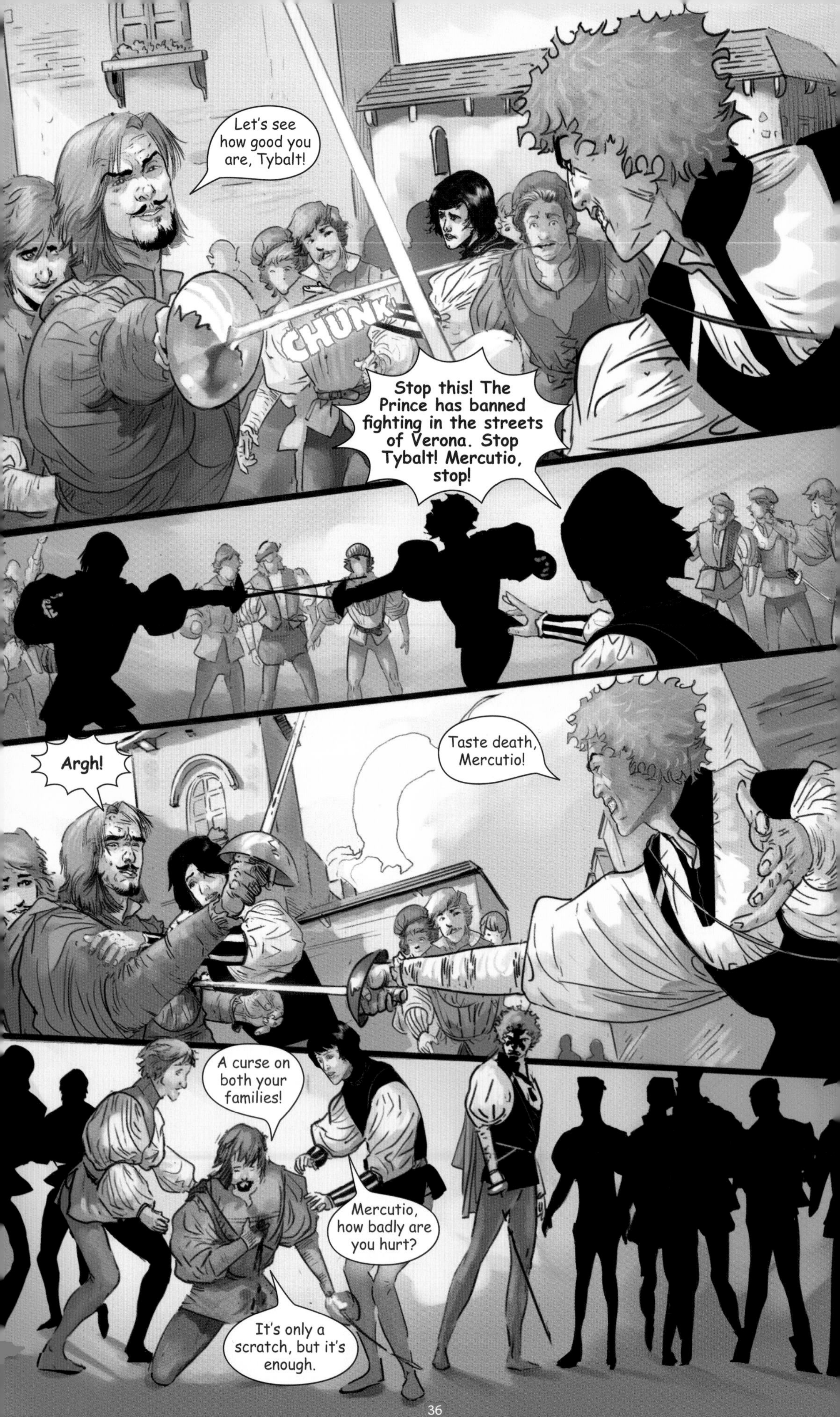
Let's see how good you are, Tybalt!
CHUNK!
Stop this! The Prince has banned fighting in the streets of Verona. Stop Tybalt! Mercutio, stop!
Argh!
Taste death, Mercutio!
A curse on both your families!
Mercutio, how badly are you hurt?
It's only a scratch, but it's enough.

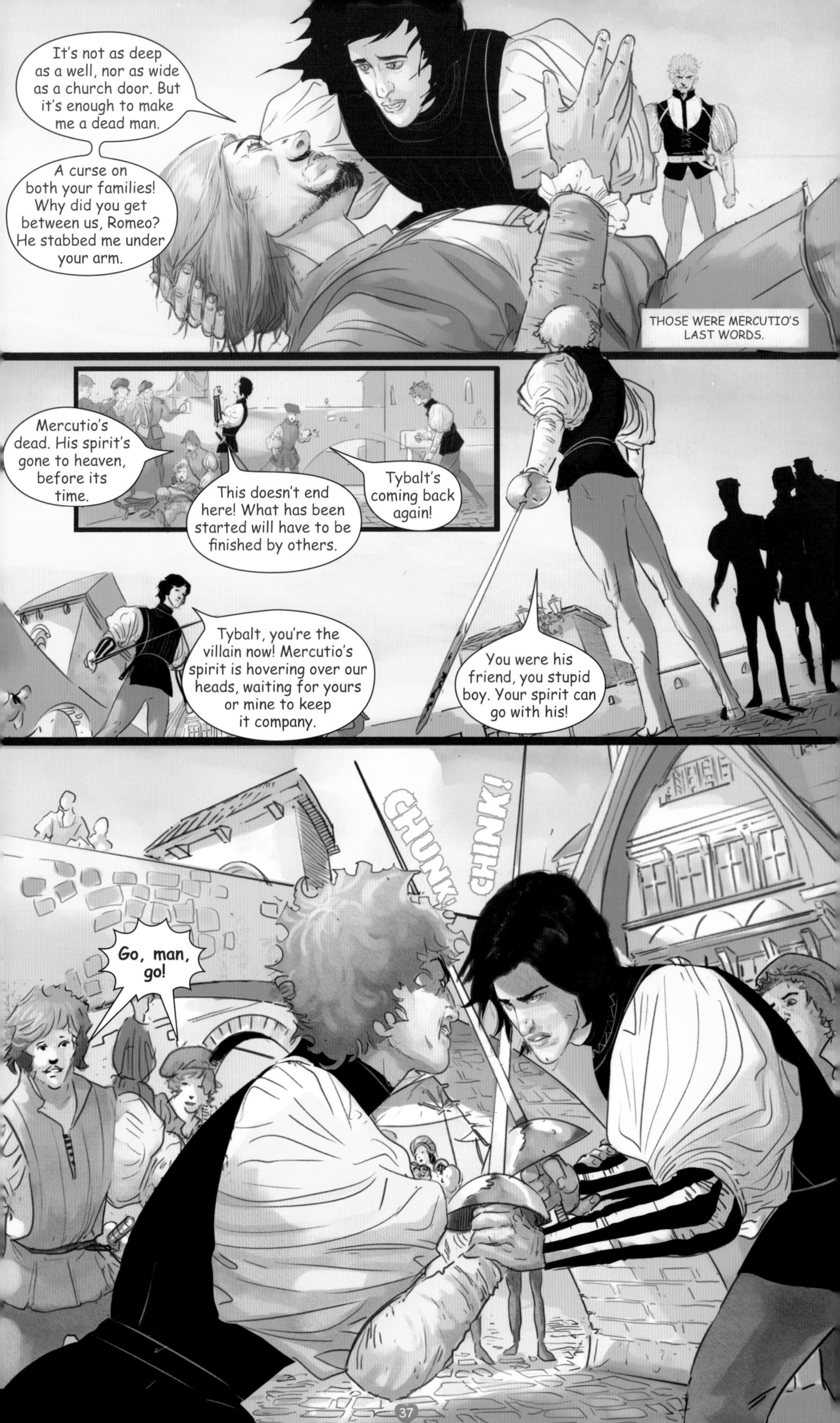
It's not as deep as a well, nor as wide as a church door. But it's enough to make me a dead man.
A curse on both your families! Why did you get between us, Romeo? He stabbed me under your arm.
THOSE WERE MERCUTIO'S LAST WORDS.
Mercutio's dead. His spirit's gone to heaven, before its time.
This doesn't end here! What has been started will have to be finished by others.
Tybalt's coming back again!
Tybalt, you're the villain now! Mercutio's spirit is hovering over our heads, waiting for yours or mine to keep it company.
You were his friend, you stupid boy. Your spirit can go with his!
CHUNK!
CHINK!
Go, man, go!

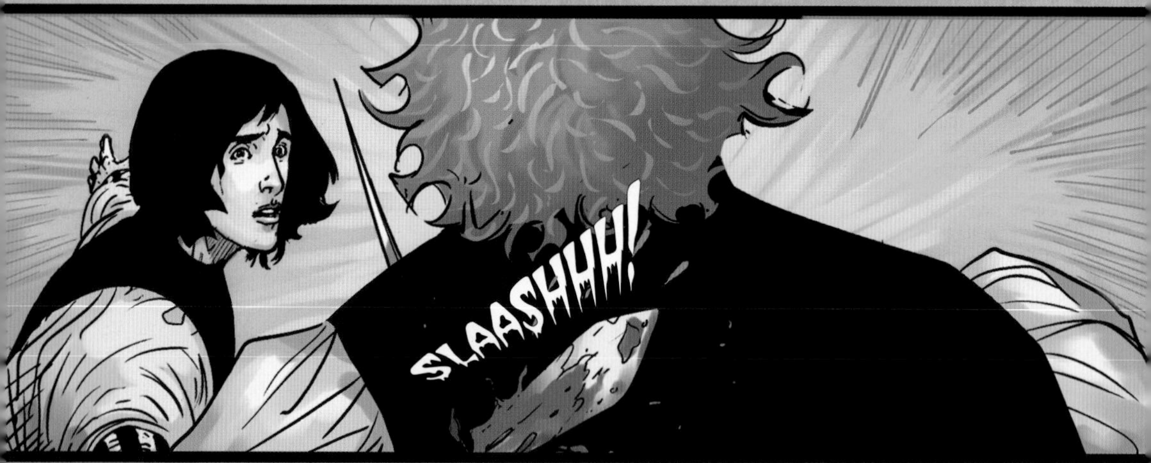
SLAASHHH!

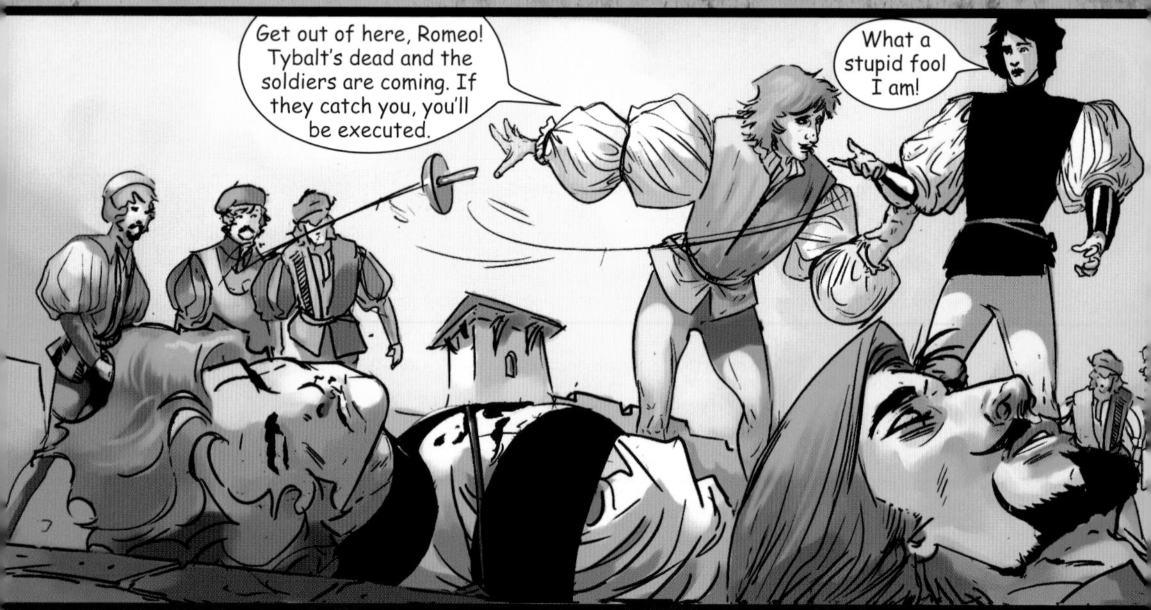
Get out of here, Romeo! Tybalt's dead and the soldiers are coming. If they catch you, you'll be executed.
What a stupid fool I am!

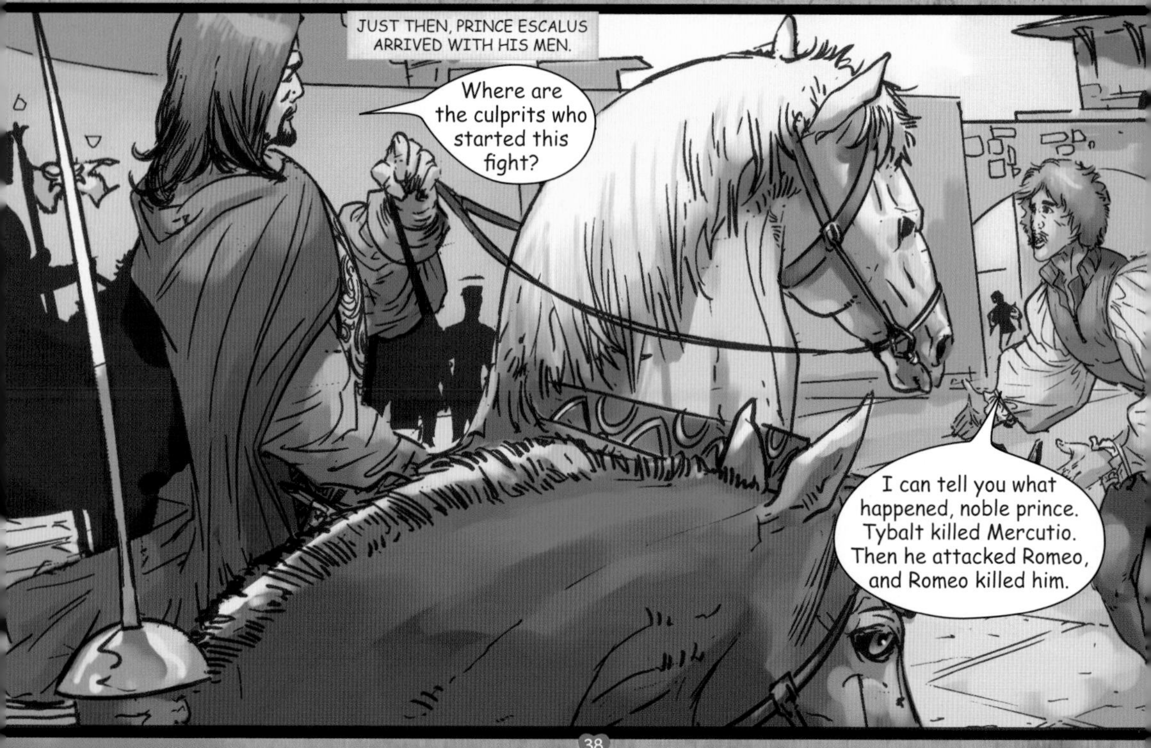
JUST THEN, PRINCE ESCALUS ARRIVED WITH HIS MEN.
Where are the culprits who started this fight?
I can tell you what happened, noble prince. Tybalt killed Mercutio. Then he attacked Romeo, and Romeo killed him.

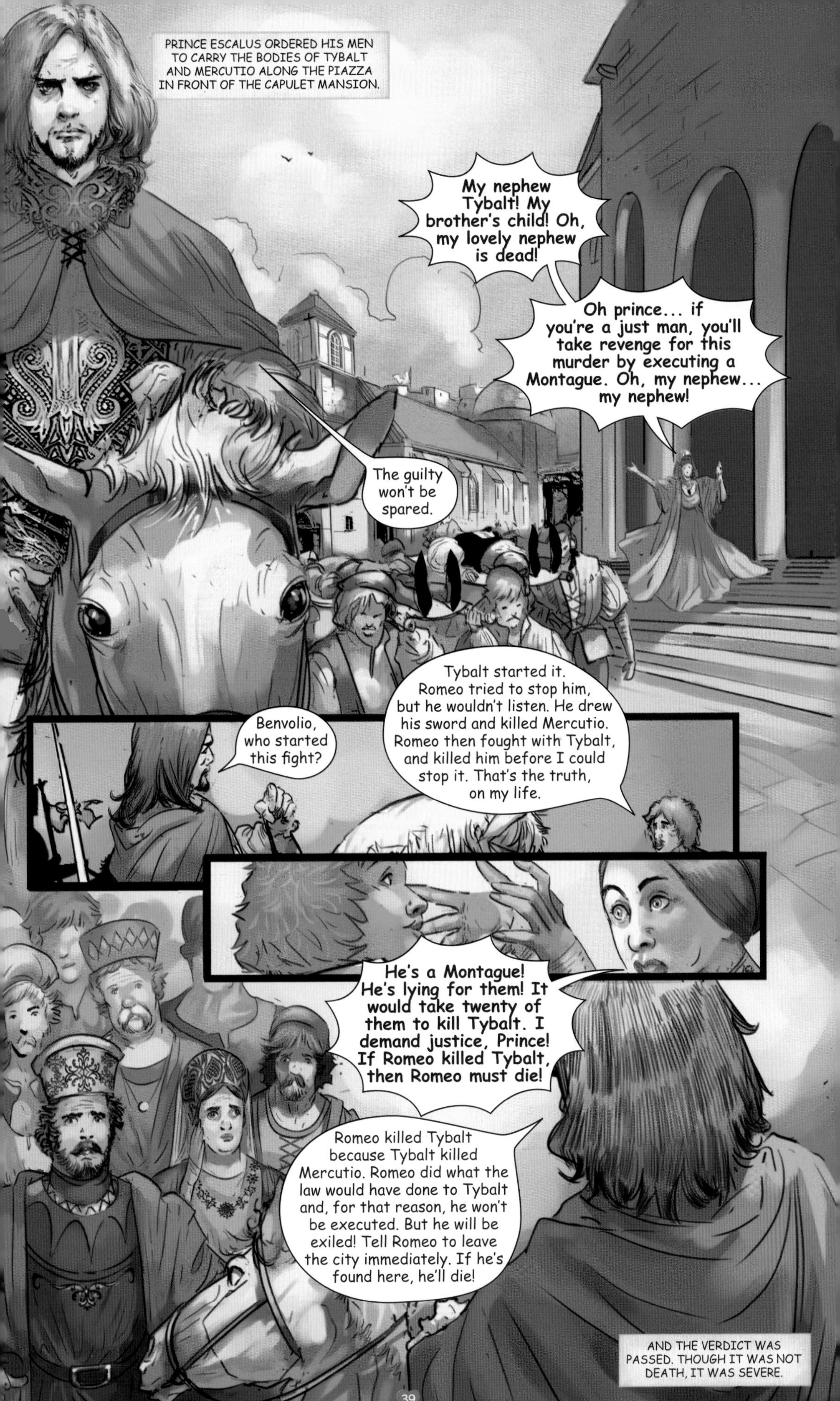
PRINCE ESCALUS ORDERED HIS MEN TO CARRY THE BODIES OF TYBALT AND MERCUTIO ALONG THE PIAZZA IN FRONT OF THE CAPULET MANSION.
My nephew Tybalt! My brother's child! Oh, my lovely nephew is dead!
Oh prince... if you're a just man, you'll take revenge for this murder by executing a Montague. Oh, my nephew... my nephew!
The guilty won't be spared.
Benvolio, who started this fight?
Tybalt started it. Romeo tried to stop him, but he wouldn't listen. He drew his sword and killed Mercutio. Romeo then fought with Tybalt, and killed him before I could stop it. That's the truth, on my life.
He's a Montague! He's lying for them! It would take twenty of them to kill Tybalt. I demand justice, Prince! If Romeo killed Tybalt, then Romeo must die!
Romeo killed Tybalt because Tybalt killed Mercutio. Romeo did what the law would have done to Tybalt and, for that reason, he won't be executed. But he will be exiled! Tell Romeo to leave the city immediately. If he's found here, he'll die!
AND THE VERDICT WAS PASSED. THOUGH IT WAS NOT DEATH, IT WAS SEVERE.

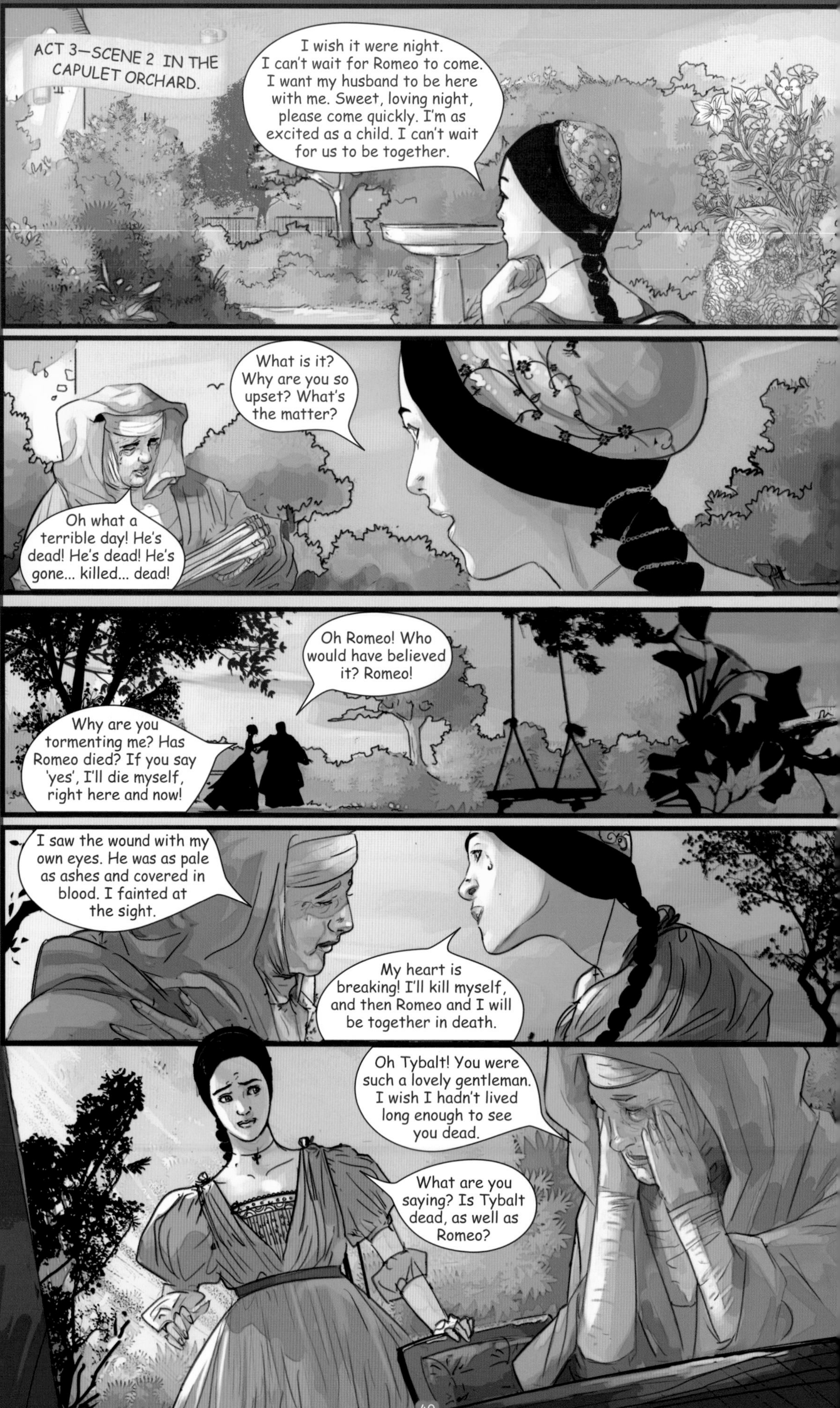
ACT 3—SCENE 2 IN THE CAPULET ORCHARD.
I wish it were night. I can't wait for Romeo to come. I want my husband to be here with me. Sweet, loving night, please come quickly. I'm as excited as a child. I can't wait for us to be together.
What is it? Why are you so upset? What's the matter?
Oh what a terrible day! He's dead! He's dead! He's gone... killed... dead!
Oh Romeo! Who would have believed it? Romeo!
Why are you tormenting me? Has Romeo died? If you say 'yes', I'll die myself, right here and now!
I saw the wound with my own eyes. He was as pale as ashes and covered in blood. I fainted at the sight.
My heart is breaking! I'll kill myself, and then Romeo and I will be together in death.
Oh Tybalt! You were such a lovely gentleman. I wish I hadn't lived long enough to see you dead.
What are you saying? Is Tybalt dead, as well as Romeo?

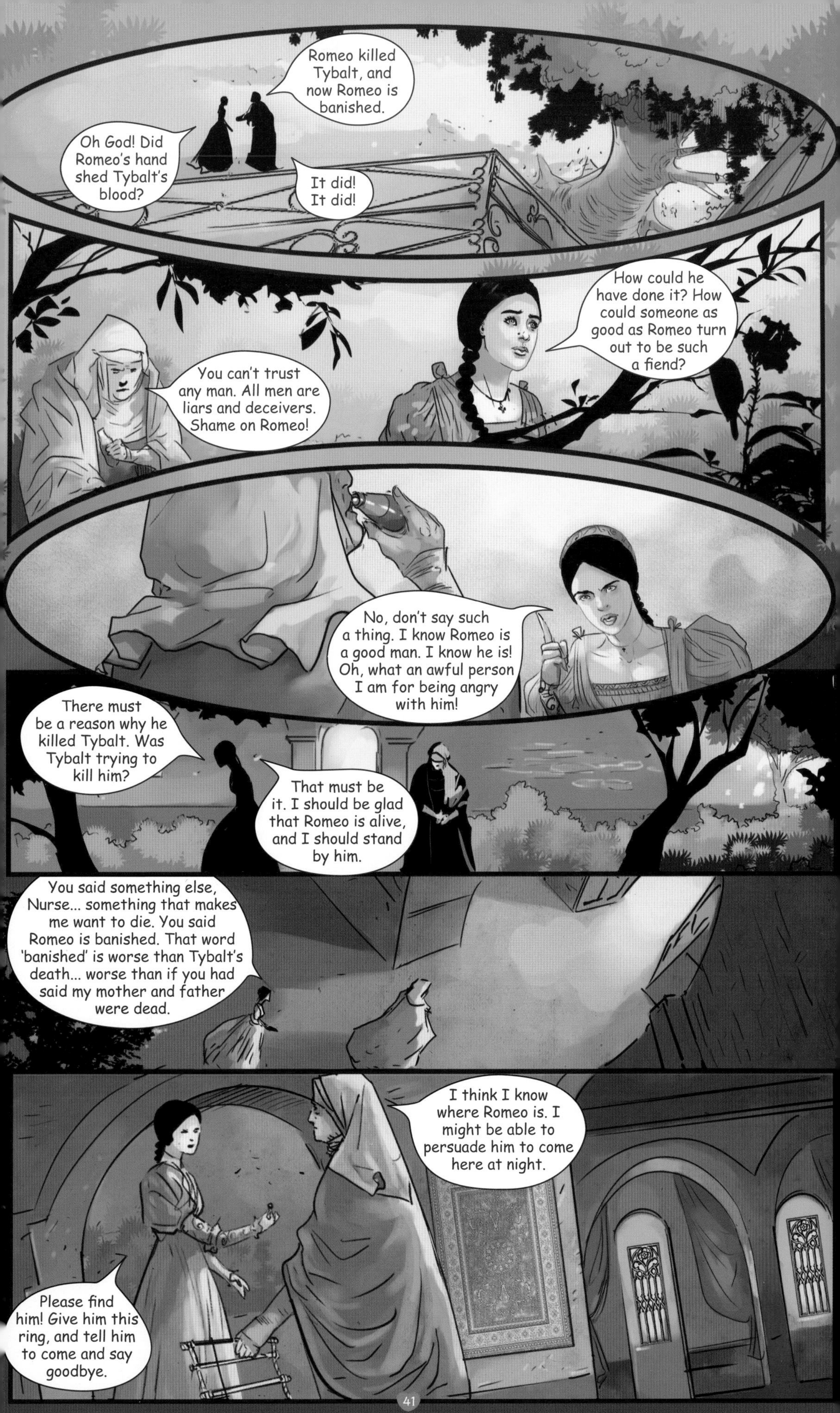

Romeo killed Tybalt, and now Romeo is banished.
Oh God! Did Romeo's hand shed Tybalt's blood?
It did! It did!
How could he have done it? How could someone as good as Romeo turn out to be such a fiend?
You can't trust any man. All men are liars and deceivers. Shame on Romeo!
No, don't say such a thing. I know Romeo is a good man. I know he is! Oh, what an awful person I am for being angry with him!
There must be a reason why he killed Tybalt. Was Tybalt trying to kill him?
That must be it. I should be glad that Romeo is alive, and I should stand by him.
You said something else, Nurse... something that makes me want to die. You said Romeo is banished. That word 'banished' is worse than Tybalt's death... worse than if you had said my mother and father were dead.
I think I know where Romeo is. I might be able to persuade him to come here at night.
Please find him! Give him this ring, and tell him to come and say goodbye.

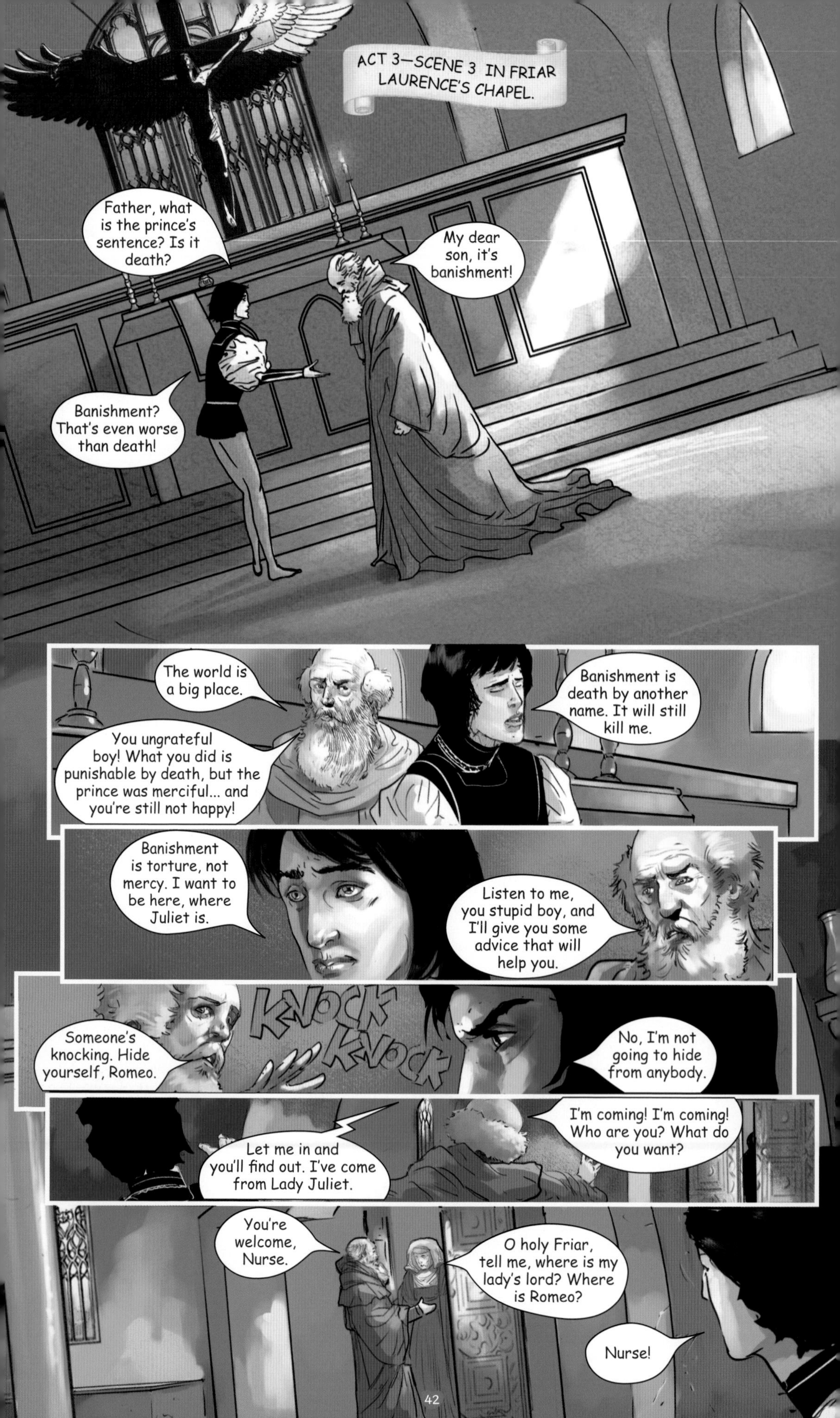
ACT 3—SCENE 3 IN FRIAR LAURENCE'S CHAPEL.
Father, what is the prince's sentence? Is it death?
My dear son, it's banishment!
Banishment? That's even worse than death!
The world is a big place.
Banishment is death by another name. It will still kill me.
You ungrateful boy! What you did is punishable by death, but the prince was merciful... and you're still not happy!
Banishment is torture, not mercy. I want to be here, where Juliet is.
Listen to me, you stupid boy, and I'll give you some advice that will help you.
KNOCK KNOCK
Someone's knocking. Hide yourself, Romeo.
No, I'm not going to hide from anybody.
I'm coming! I'm coming! Who are you? What do you want?
Let me in and you'll find out. I've come from Lady Juliet.
You're welcome, Nurse.
O holy Friar, tell me, where is my lady's lord? Where is Romeo?
Nurse!

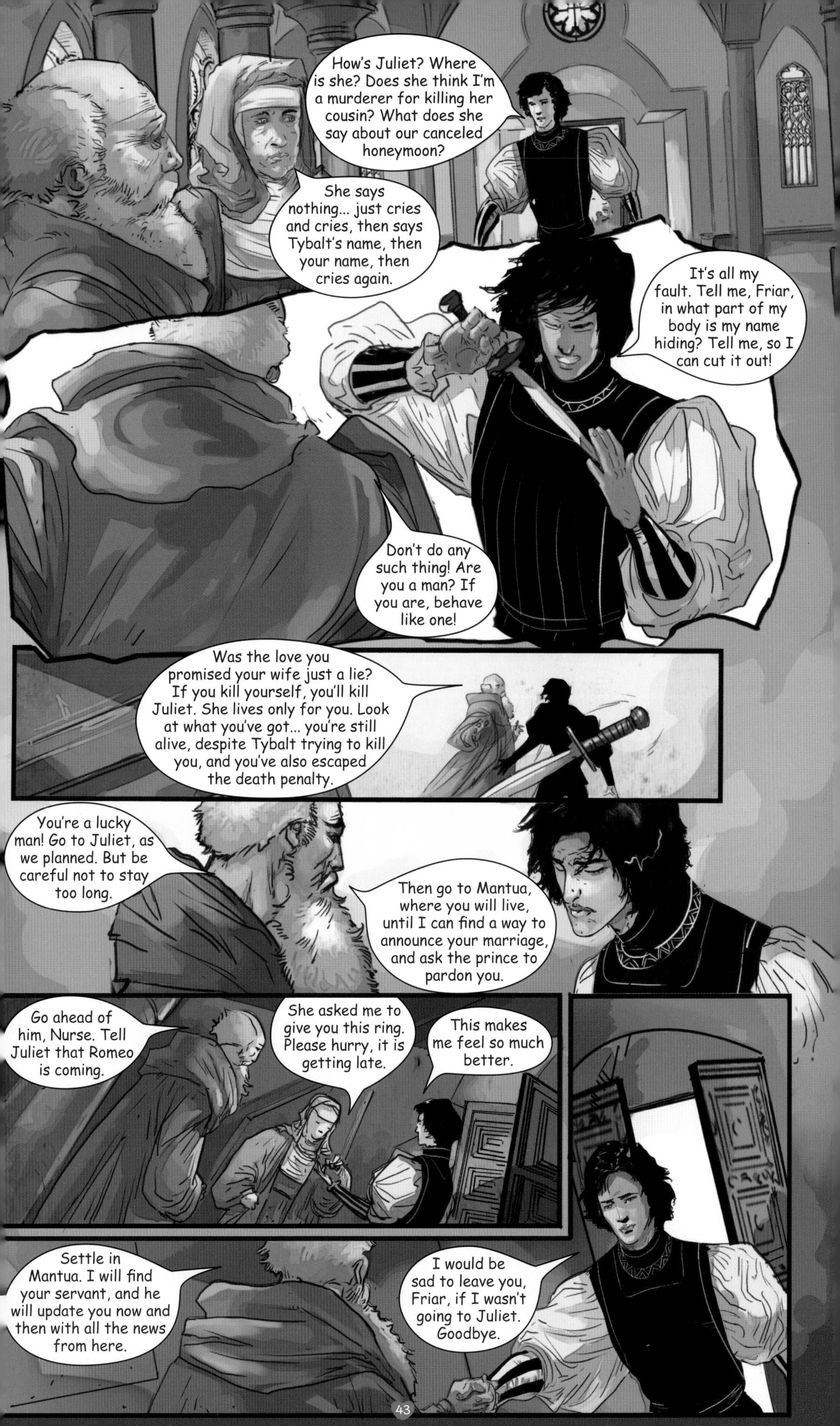
How's Juliet? Where is she? Does she think I'm a murderer for killing her cousin? What does she say about our canceled honeymoon?
She says nothing... just cries and cries, then says Tybalt's name, then your name, then cries again.
It's all my fault. Tell me, Friar, in what part of my body is my name hiding? Tell me, so I can cut it out!
Don't do any such thing! Are you a man? If you are, behave like one!
Was the love you promised your wife just a lie? If you kill yourself, you'll kill Juliet. She lives only for you. Look at what you've got... you're still alive, despite Tybalt trying to kill you, and you've also escaped the death penalty.
You're a lucky man! Go to Juliet, as we planned. But be careful not to stay too long.
Then go to Mantua, where you will live, until I can find a way to announce your marriage, and ask the prince to pardon you.
Go ahead of him, Nurse. Tell Juliet that Romeo is coming.
She asked me to give you this ring. Please hurry, it is getting late.
This makes me feel so much better.
Settle in Mantua. I will find your servant, and he will update you now and then with all the news from here.
I would be sad to leave you, Friar, if I wasn't going to Juliet. Goodbye.

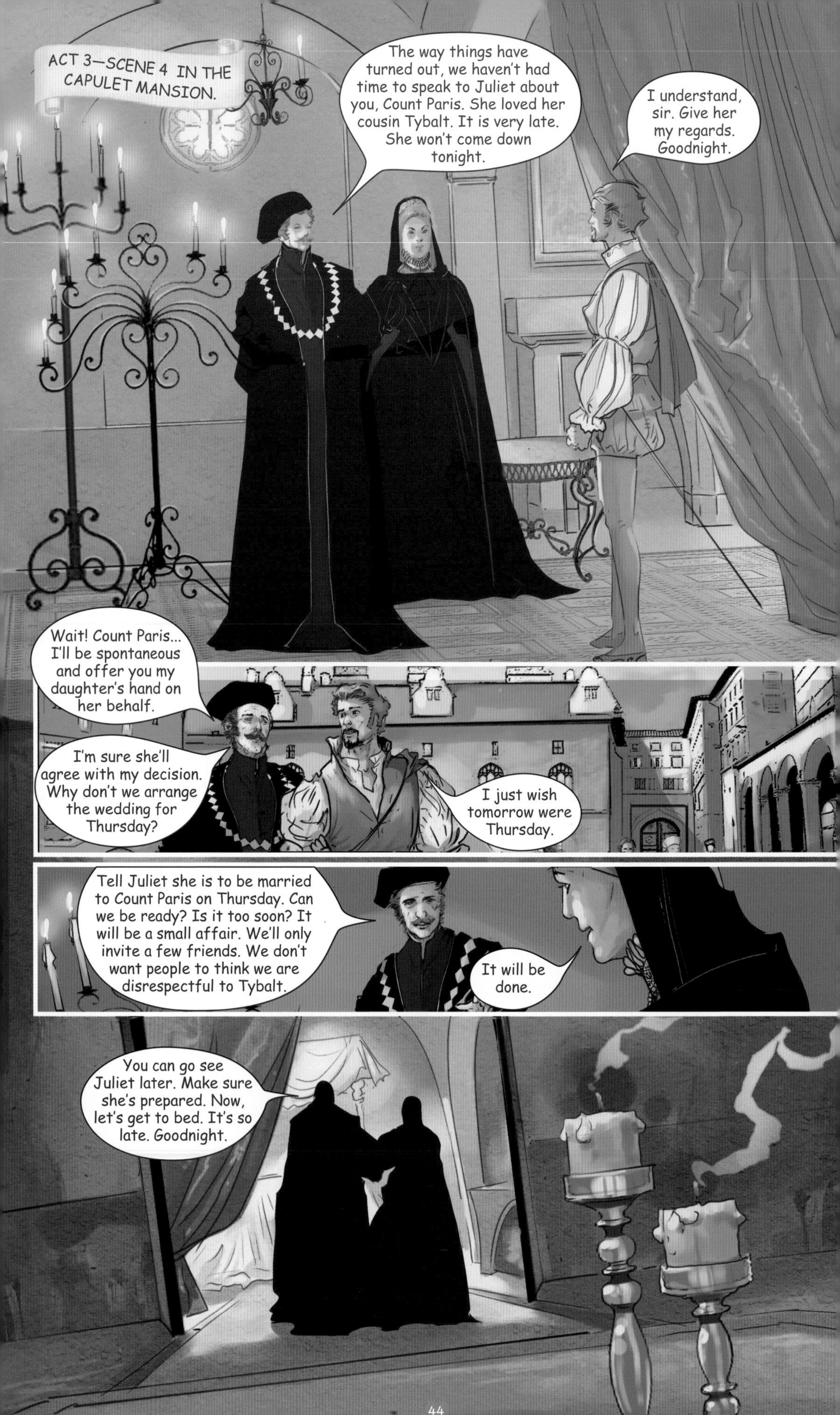
ACT 3—SCENE 4 IN THE CAPULET MANSION.
The way things have turned out, we haven't had time to speak to Juliet about you, Count Paris. She loved her cousin Tybalt. It is very late. She won't come down tonight.
I understand, sir. Give her my regards. Goodnight.
Wait! Count Paris... I'll be spontaneous and offer you my daughter's hand on her behalf.
I'm sure she'll agree with my decision. Why don't we arrange the wedding for Thursday?
I just wish tomorrow were Thursday.
Tell Juliet she is to be married to Count Paris on Thursday. Can we be ready? Is it too soon? It will be a small affair. We'll only invite a few friends. We don't want people to think we are disrespectful to Tybalt.
It will be done.
You can go see Juliet later. Make sure she's prepared. Now, let's get to bed. It's so late. Goodnight.

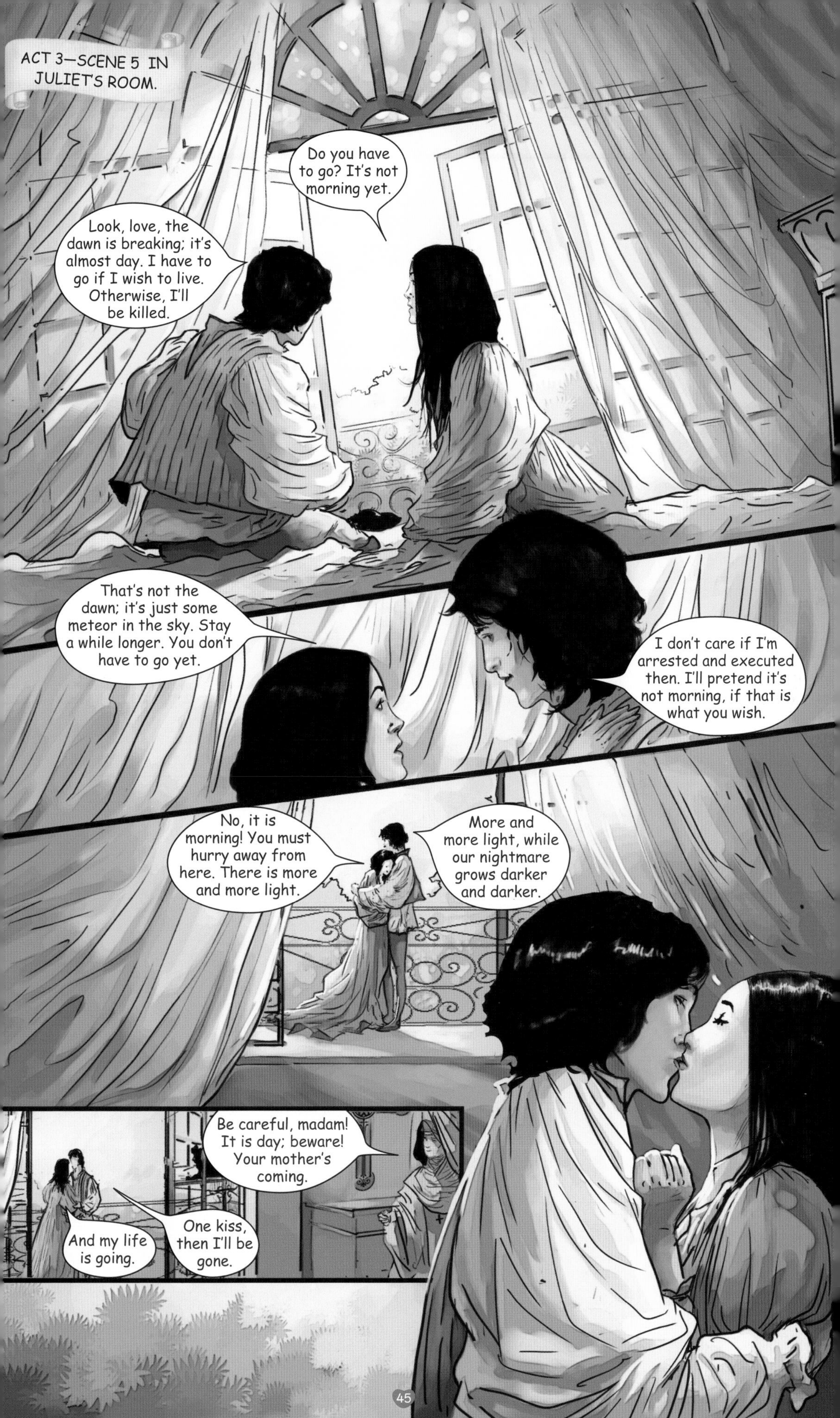
ACT 3—SCENE 5 IN JULIET'S ROOM.
Do you have to go? It's not morning yet.
Look, love, the dawn is breaking; it's almost day. I have to go if I wish to live. Otherwise, I'll be killed.
That's not the dawn; it's just some meteor in the sky. Stay a while longer. You don't have to go yet.
I don't care if I'm arrested and executed then. I'll pretend it's not morning, if that is what you wish.
No, it is morning! You must hurry away from here. There is more and more light.
More and more light, while our nightmare grows darker and darker.
Be careful, madam! It is day; beware! Your mother's coming.
One kiss, then I'll be gone.
And my life is going.

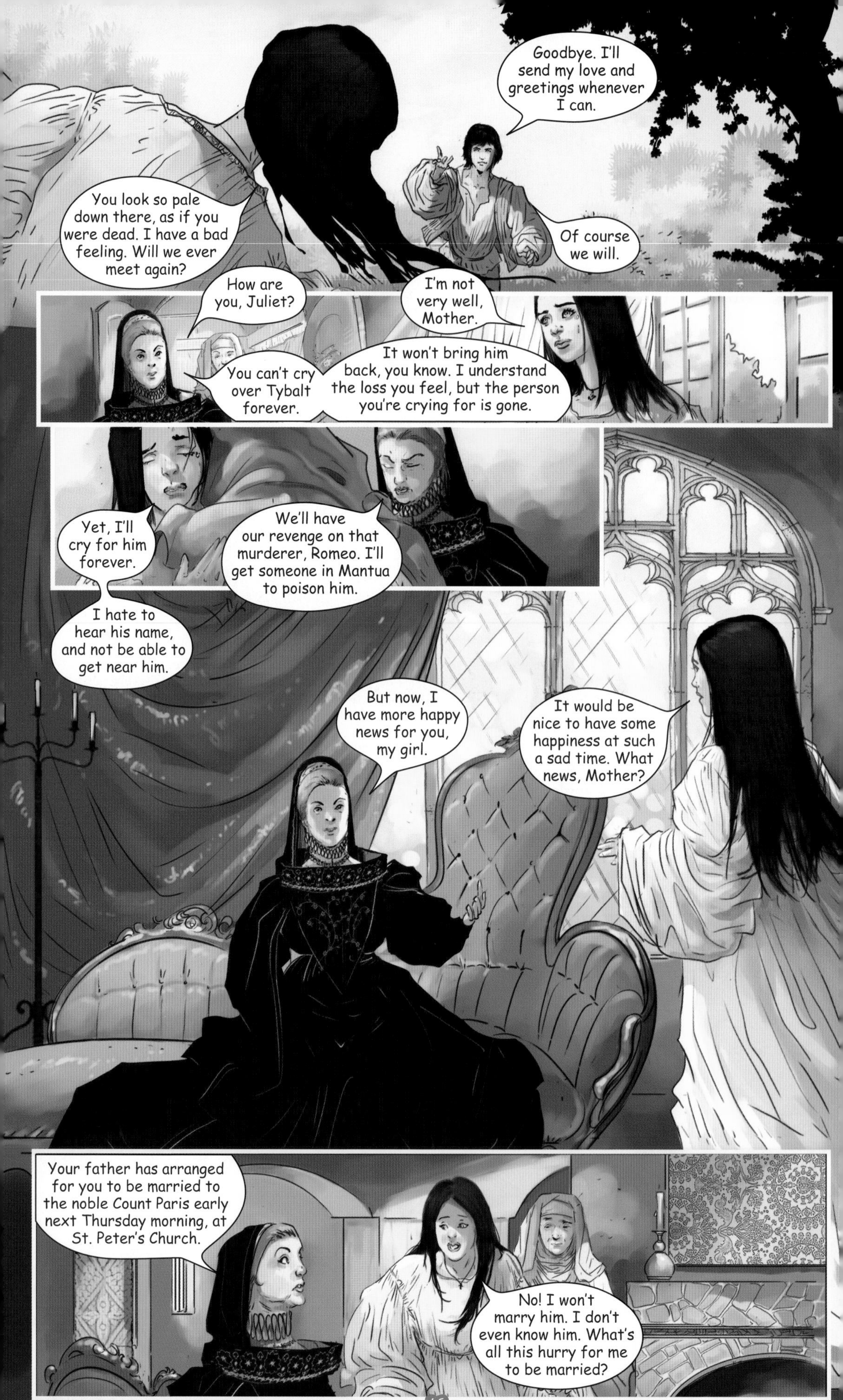
Goodbye. I'll send my love and greetings whenever I can.
You look so pale down there, as if you were dead. I have a bad feeling. Will we ever meet again?
Of course we will.
How are you, Juliet?
I'm not very well, Mother.
You can't cry over Tybalt forever.
It won't bring him back, you know. I understand the loss you feel, but the person you're crying for is gone.
Yet, I'll cry for him forever.
We'll have our revenge on that murderer, Romeo. I'll get someone in Mantua to poison him.
I hate to hear his name, and not be able to get near him.
But now, I have more happy news for you, my girl.
It would be nice to have some happiness at such a sad time. What news, Mother?
Your father has arranged for you to be married to the noble Count Paris early next Thursday morning, at St. Peter's Church.
No! I won't marry him. I don't even know him. What's all this hurry for me to be married?

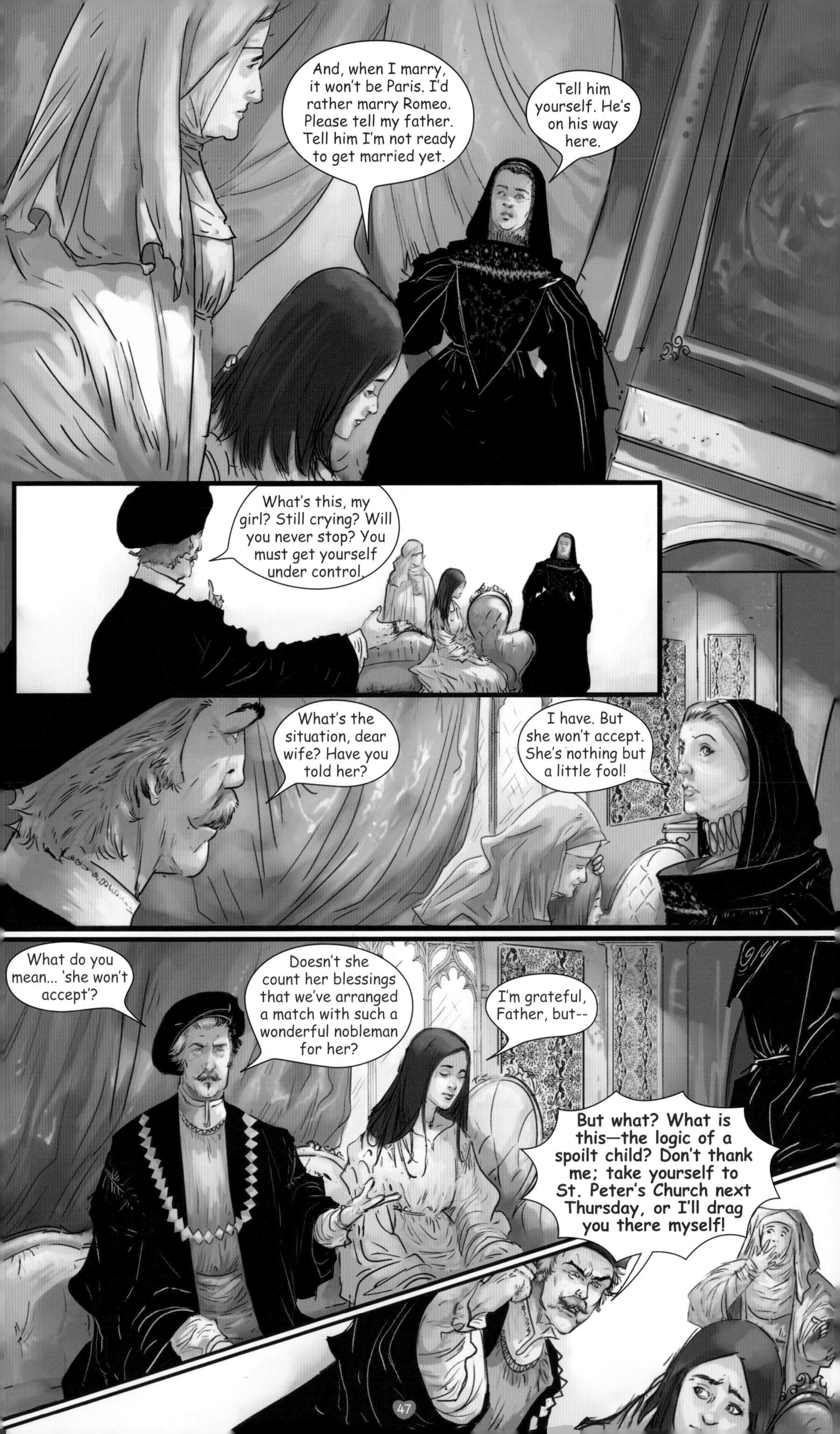
And, when I marry, it won't be Paris. I'd rather marry Romeo. Please tell my father. Tell him I'm not ready to get married yet.
Tell him yourself. He's on his way here.
What's this, my girl? Still crying? Will you never stop? You must get yourself under control.
What's the situation, dear wife? Have you told her?
I have. But she won't accept. She's nothing but a little fool!
What do you mean... 'she won't accept'?
Doesn't she count her blessings that we've arranged a match with such a wonderful nobleman for her?
I'm grateful, Father, but--
But what? What is this—the logic of a spoilt child? Don't thank me; take yourself to St. Peter's Church next Thursday, or I'll drag you there myself!

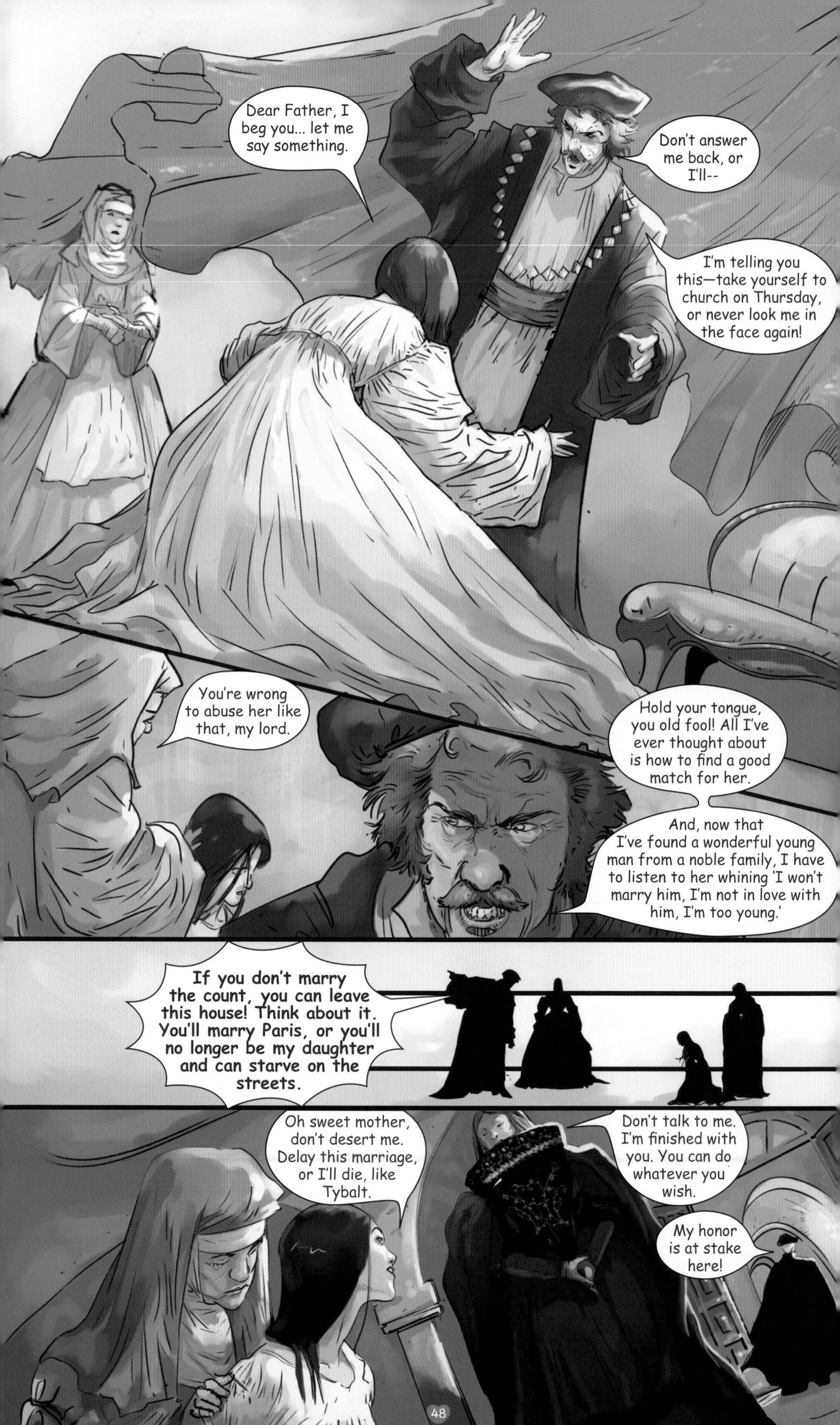

Dear Father, I beg you... let me say something.
Don't answer me back, or I'll--
I'm telling you this—take yourself to church on Thursday, or never look me in the face again!
You're wrong to abuse her like that, my lord.
Hold your tongue, you old fool! All I've ever thought about is how to find a good match for her.
And, now that I've found a wonderful young man from a noble family, I have to listen to her whining 'I won't marry him, I'm not in love with him, I'm too young.'
If you don't marry the count, you can leave this house! Think about it. You'll marry Paris, or you'll no longer be my daughter and can starve on the streets.
Oh sweet mother, don't desert me. Delay this marriage, or I'll die, like Tybalt.
Don't talk to me. I'm finished with you. You can do whatever you wish.
My honor is at stake here!

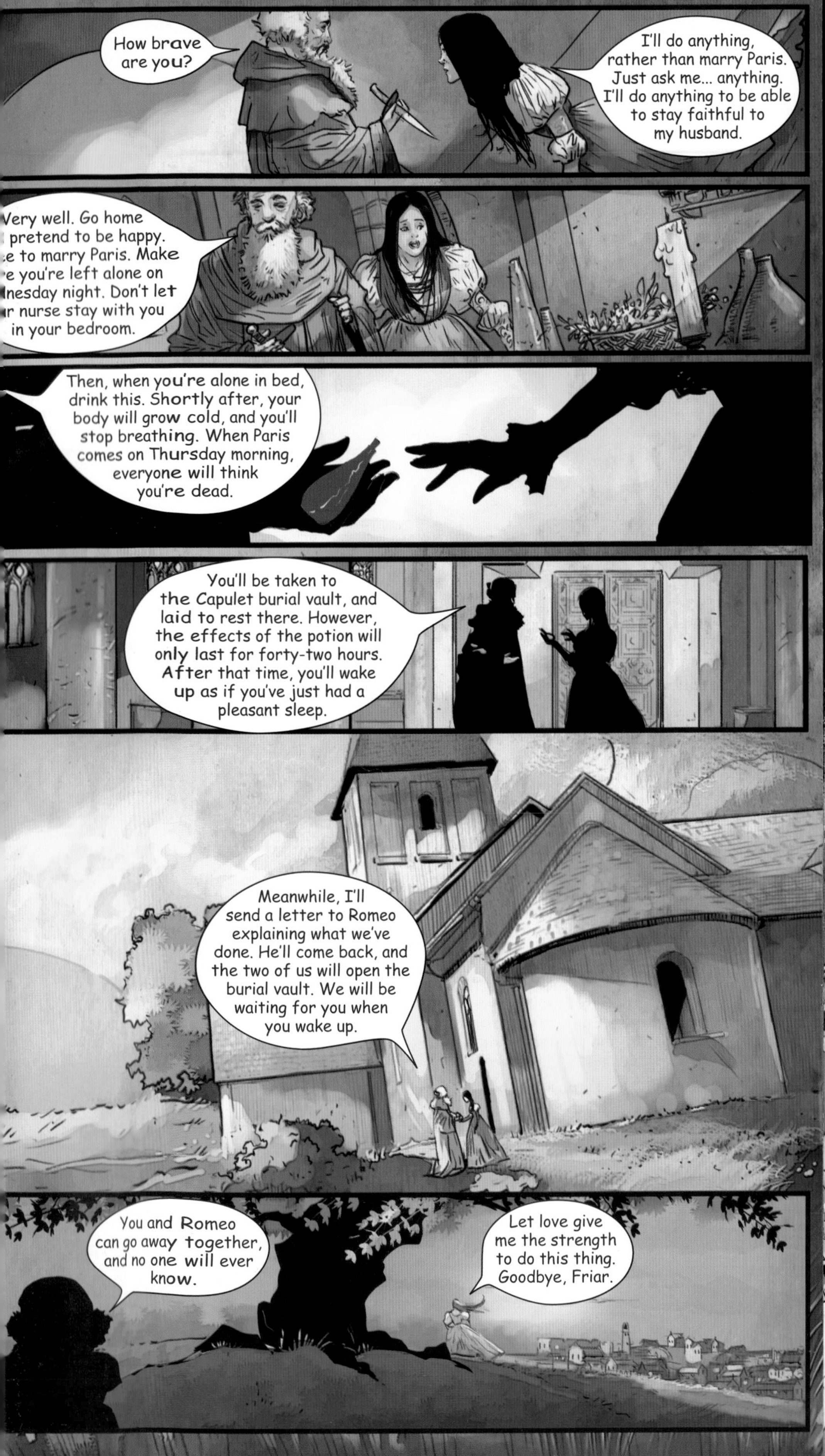
How brave are you?
I'll do anything, rather than marry Paris. Just ask me... anything. I'll do anything to be able to stay faithful to my husband.
Very well. Go home pretend to be happy. e to marry Paris. Make e you're left alone on nesday night. Don't let r nurse stay with you in your bedroom.
Then, when you're alone in bed, drink this. Shortly after, your body will grow cold, and you'll stop breathing. When Paris comes on Thursday morning, everyone will think you're dead.
You'll be taken to the Capulet burial vault, and laid to rest there. However, the effects of the potion will only last for forty-two hours. After that time, you'll wake up as if you've just had a pleasant sleep.
Meanwhile, I'll send a letter to Romeo explaining what we've done. He'll come back, and the two of us will open the burial vault. We will be waiting for you when you wake up.
You and Romeo can go away together, and no one will ever know.
Let love give me the strength to do this thing. Goodbye, Friar.

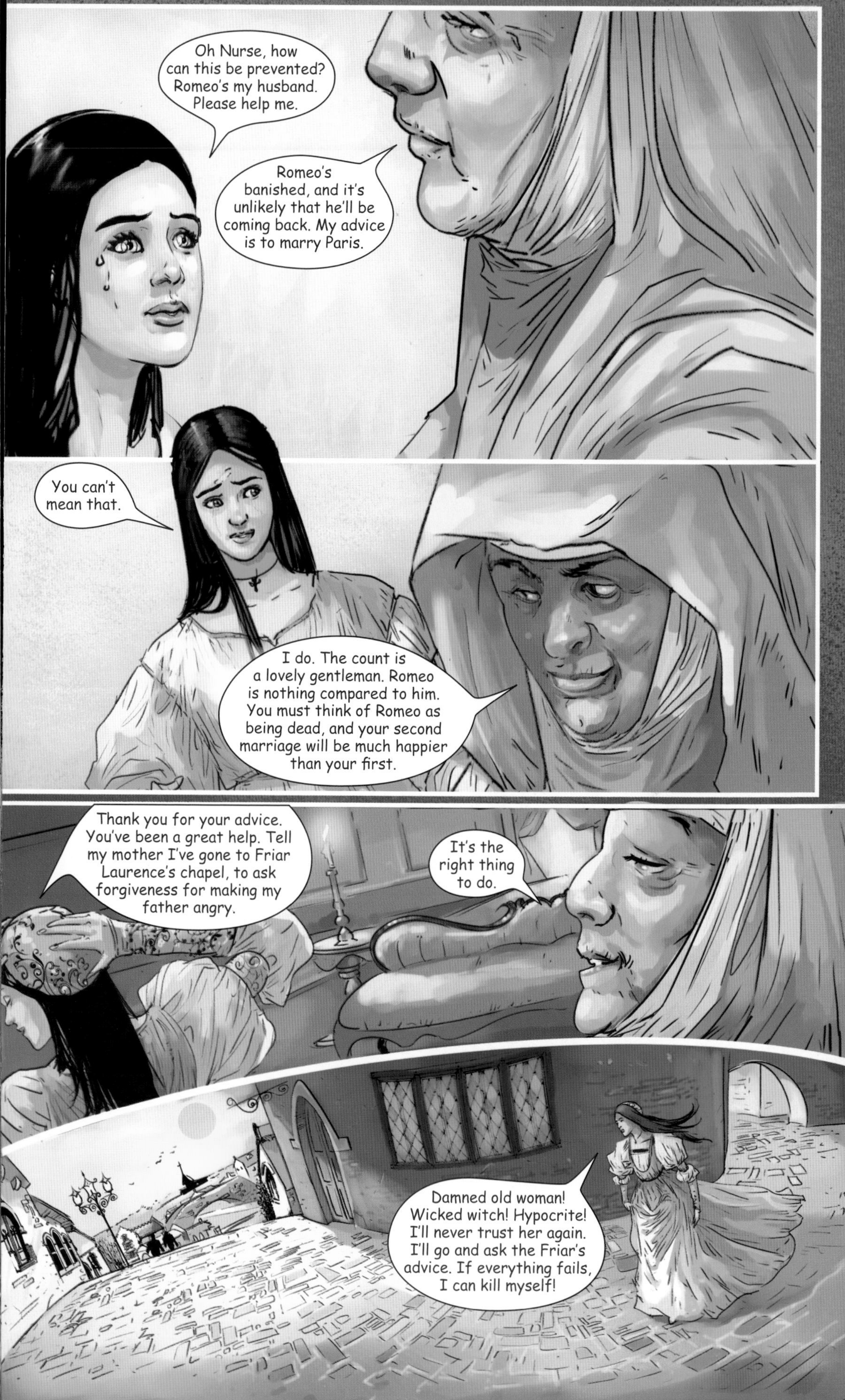
Oh Nurse, how can this be prevented? Romeo's my husband. Please help me.
Romeo's banished, and it's unlikely that he'll be coming back. My advice is to marry Paris.
You can't mean that.
I do. The count is a lovely gentleman. Romeo is nothing compared to him. You must think of Romeo as being dead, and your second marriage will be much happier than your first.
Thank you for your advice. You've been a great help. Tell my mother I've gone to Friar Laurence's chapel, to ask forgiveness for making my father angry.
It's the right thing to do.
Damned old woman! Wicked witch! Hypocrite! I'll never trust her again. I'll go and ask the Friar's advice. If everything fails, I can kill myself!

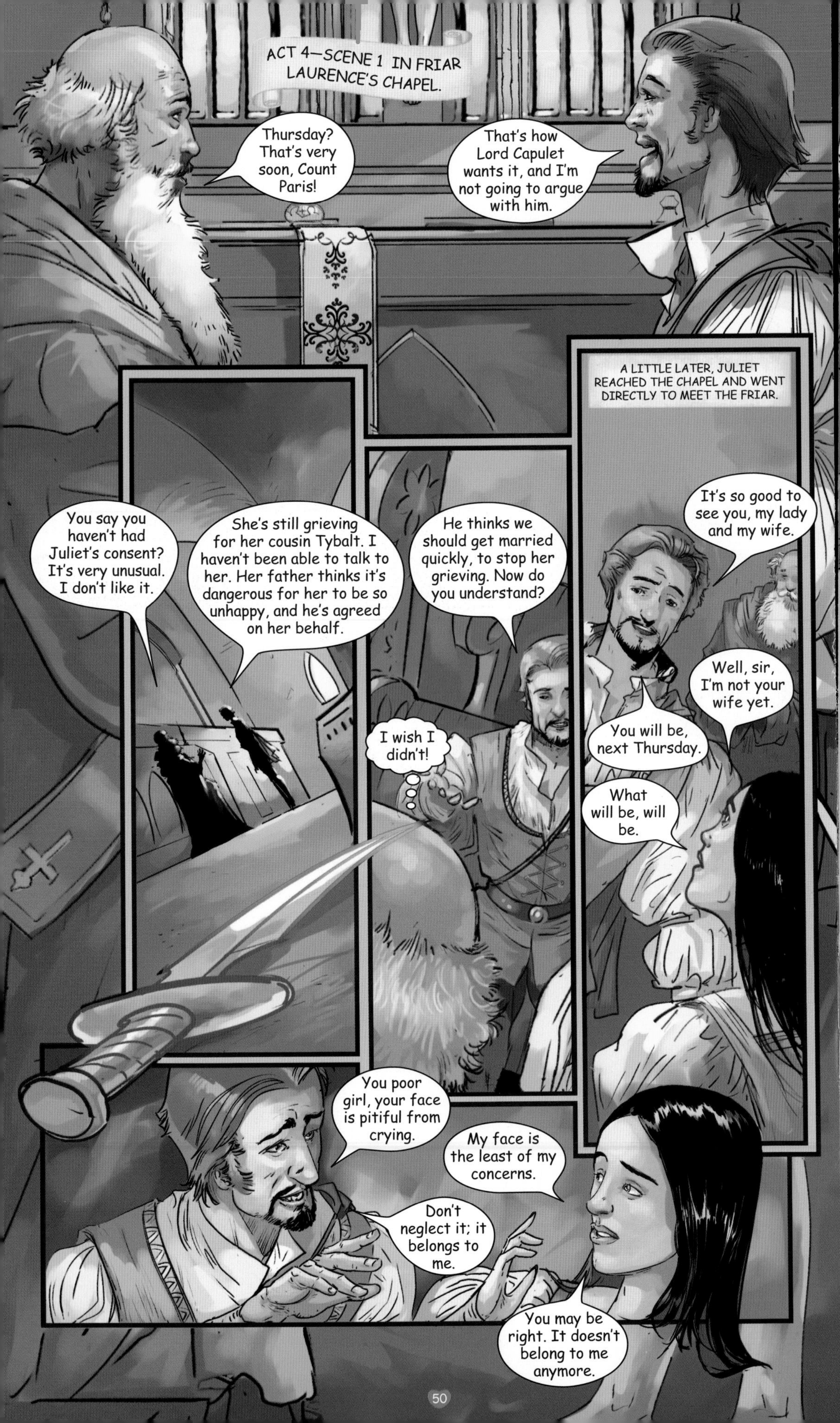
ACT 4—SCENE 1 IN FRIAR LAURENCE'S CHAPEL.
Thursday? That's very soon, Count Paris!
That's how Lord Capulet wants it, and I'm not going to argue with him.
You say you haven't had Juliet's consent? It's very unusual. I don't like it.
She's still grieving for her cousin Tybalt. I haven't been able to talk to her. Her father thinks it's dangerous for her to be so unhappy, and he's agreed on her behalf.
He thinks we should get married quickly, to stop her grieving. Now do you understand?
I wish I didn't!
A LITTLE LATER, JULIET REACHED THE CHAPEL AND WENT DIRECTLY TO MEET THE FRIAR.
It's so good to see you, my lady and my wife.
Well, sir, I'm not your wife yet.
You will be, next Thursday.
What will be, will be.
You poor girl, your face is pitiful from crying.
My face is the least of my concerns.
Don't neglect it; it belongs to me.
You may be right. It doesn't belong to me anymore.

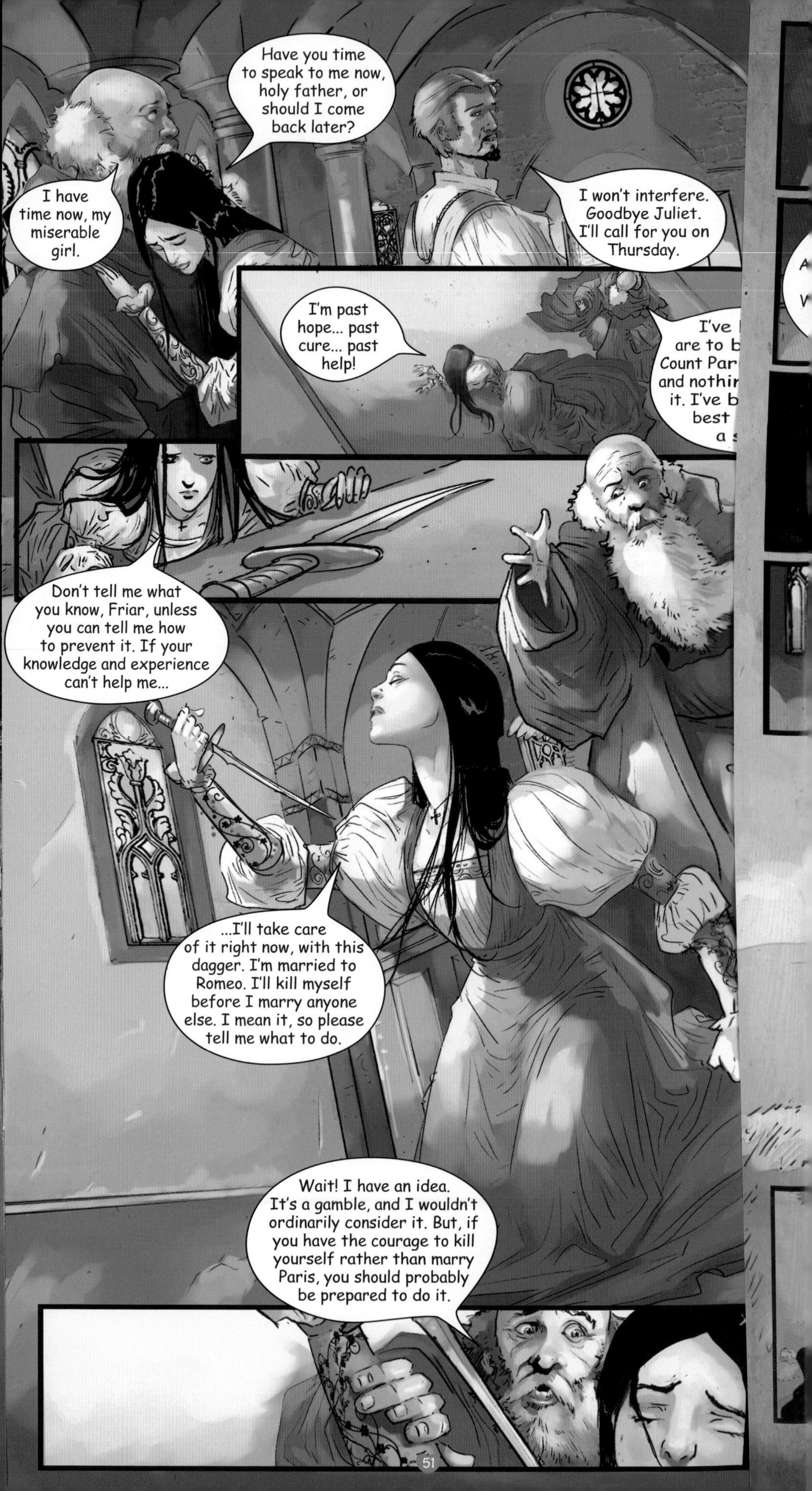
Have you time to speak to me now, holy father, or should I come back later?
I have time now, my miserable girl.
I won't interfere. Goodbye Juliet. I'll call for you on Thursday.
I'm past hope... past cure... past help!
Don't tell me what you know, Friar, unless you can tell me how to prevent it. If your knowledge and experience can't help me...
...I'll take care of it right now, with this dagger. I'm married to Romeo. I'll kill myself before I marry anyone else. I mean it, so please tell me what to do.
Wait! I have an idea. It's a gamble, and I wouldn't ordinarily consider it. But, if you have the courage to kill yourself rather than marry Paris, you should probably be prepared to do it.

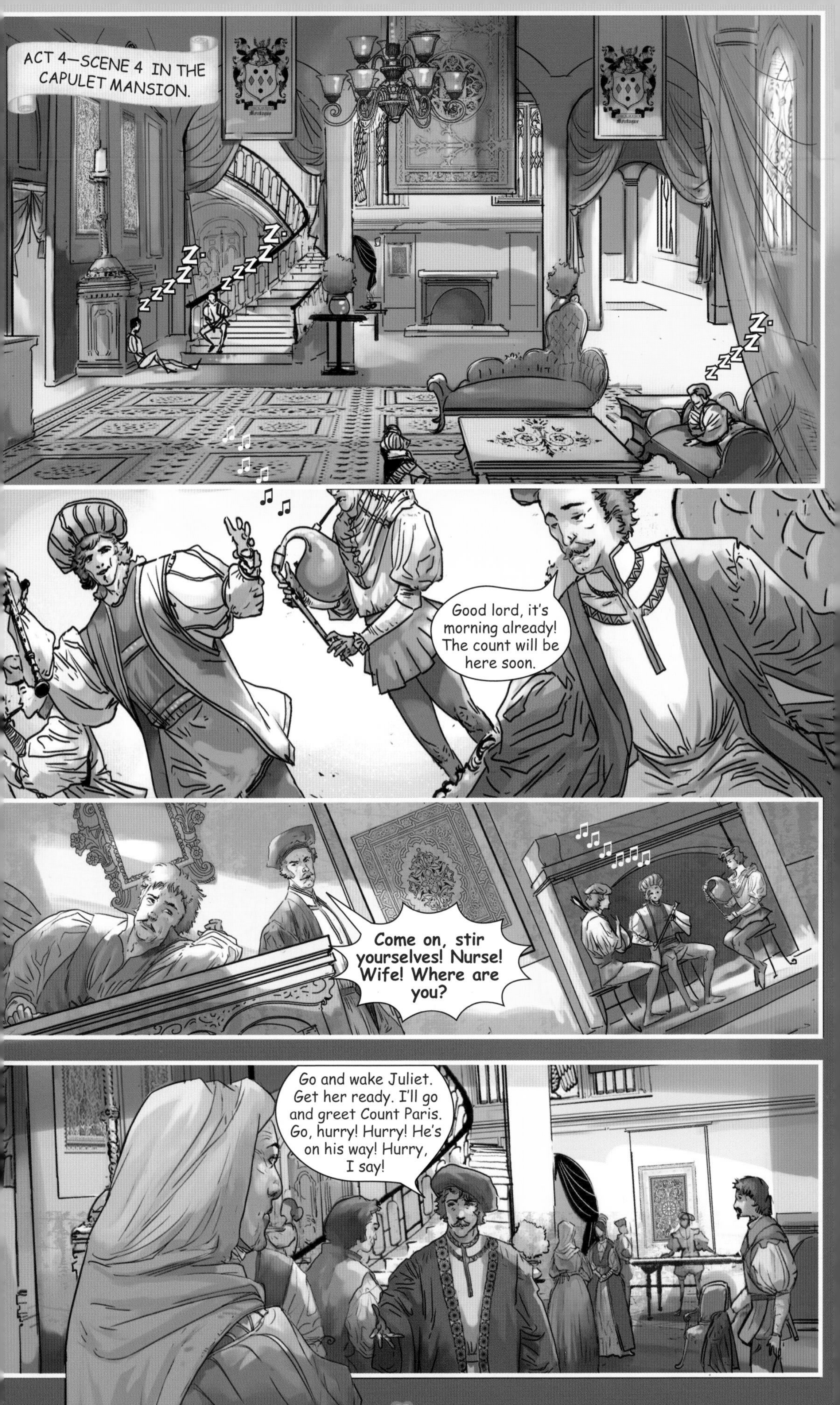
ACT 4—SCENE 4 IN THE CAPULET MANSION.
Montague
Montague
Z-Z-Z-Z
Z-Z-Z-Z-Z-Z
Z-Z-Z-Z
Good lord, it's morning already! The count will be here soon.
Come on, stir yourselves! Nurse! Wife! Where are you?
Go and wake Juliet. Get her ready. I'll go and greet Count Paris. Go, hurry! Hurry! He's on his way! Hurry, I say!

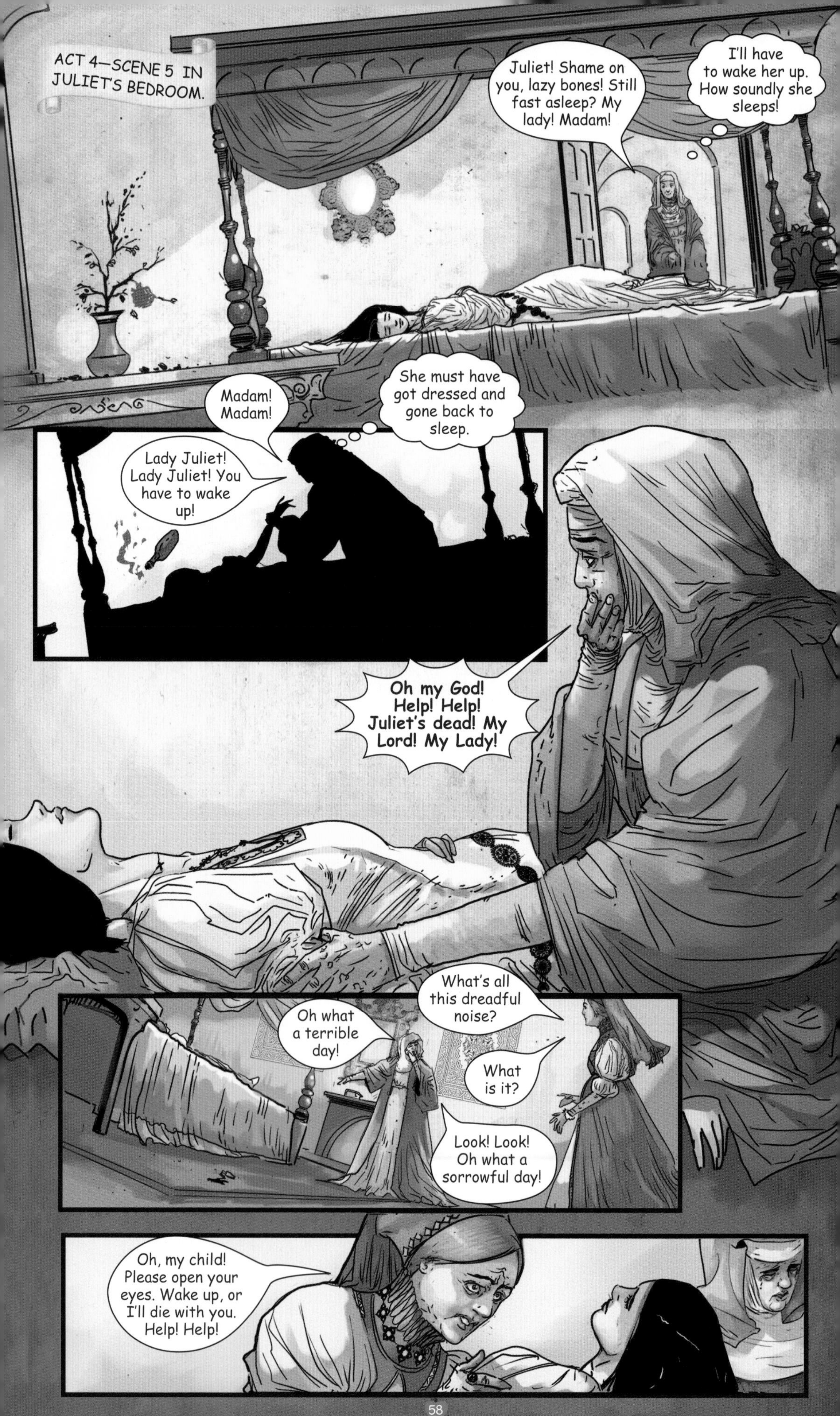
ACT 4—SCENE 5 IN JULIET'S BEDROOM.
Juliet! Shame on you, lazy bones! Still fast asleep? My lady! Madam!
I'll have to wake her up. How soundly she sleeps!
Madam! Madam!
She must have got dressed and gone back to sleep.
Lady Juliet! Lady Juliet! You have to wake up!
Oh my God! Help! Help! Juliet's dead! My Lord! My Lady!
What's all this dreadful noise?
Oh what a terrible day!
What is it?
Look! Look! Oh what a sorrowful day!
Oh, my child! Please open your eyes. Wake up, or I'll die with you. Help! Help!

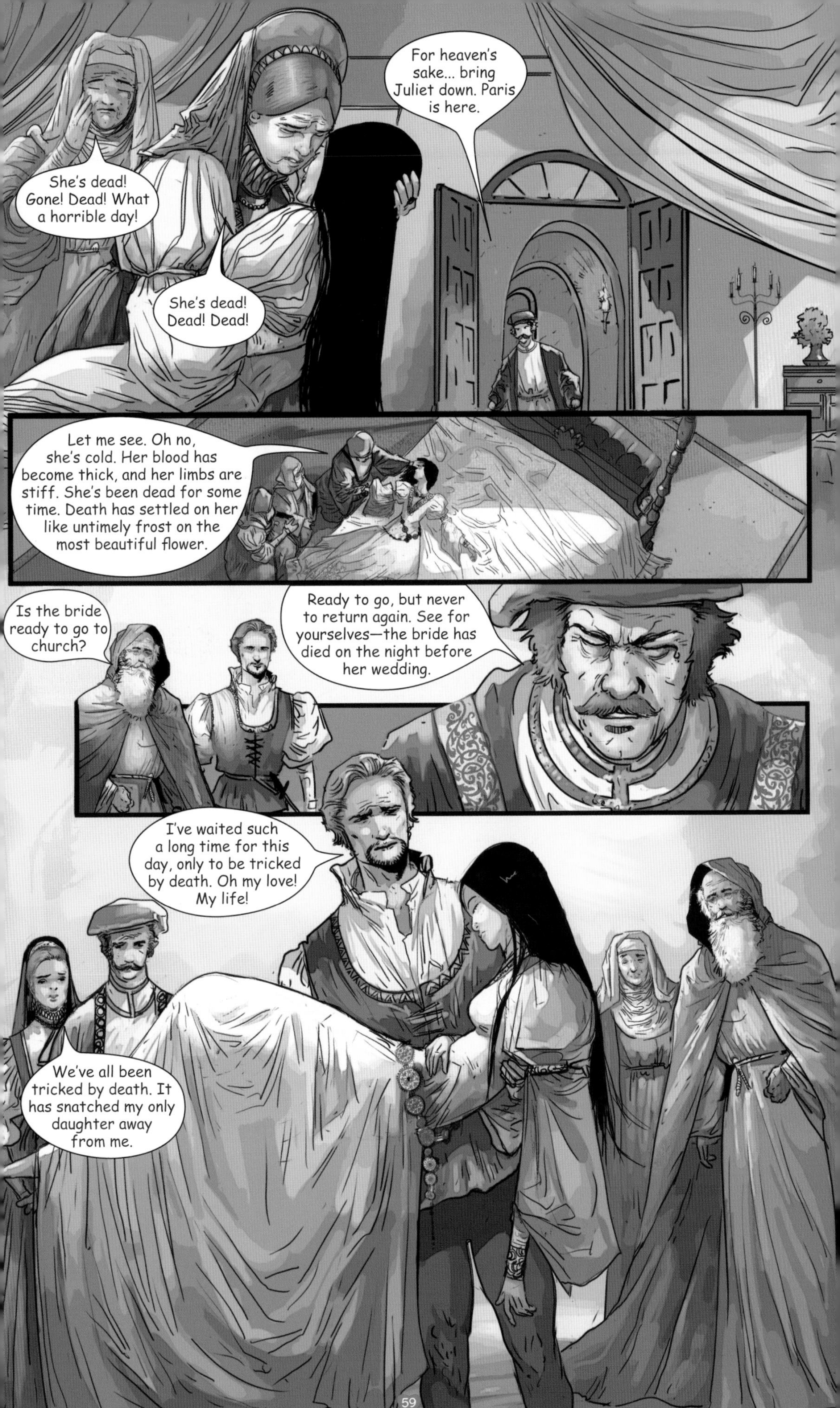
She's dead! Gone! Dead! What a horrible day!
She's dead! Dead! Dead!
For heaven's sake... bring Juliet down. Paris is here.
Let me see. Oh no, she's cold. Her blood has become thick, and her limbs are stiff. She's been dead for some time. Death has settled on her like untimely frost on the most beautiful flower.
Is the bride ready to go to church?
Ready to go, but never to return again. See for yourselves—the bride has died on the night before her wedding.
I've waited such a long time for this day, only to be tricked by death. Oh my love! My life!
We've all been tricked by death. It has snatched my only daughter away from me.

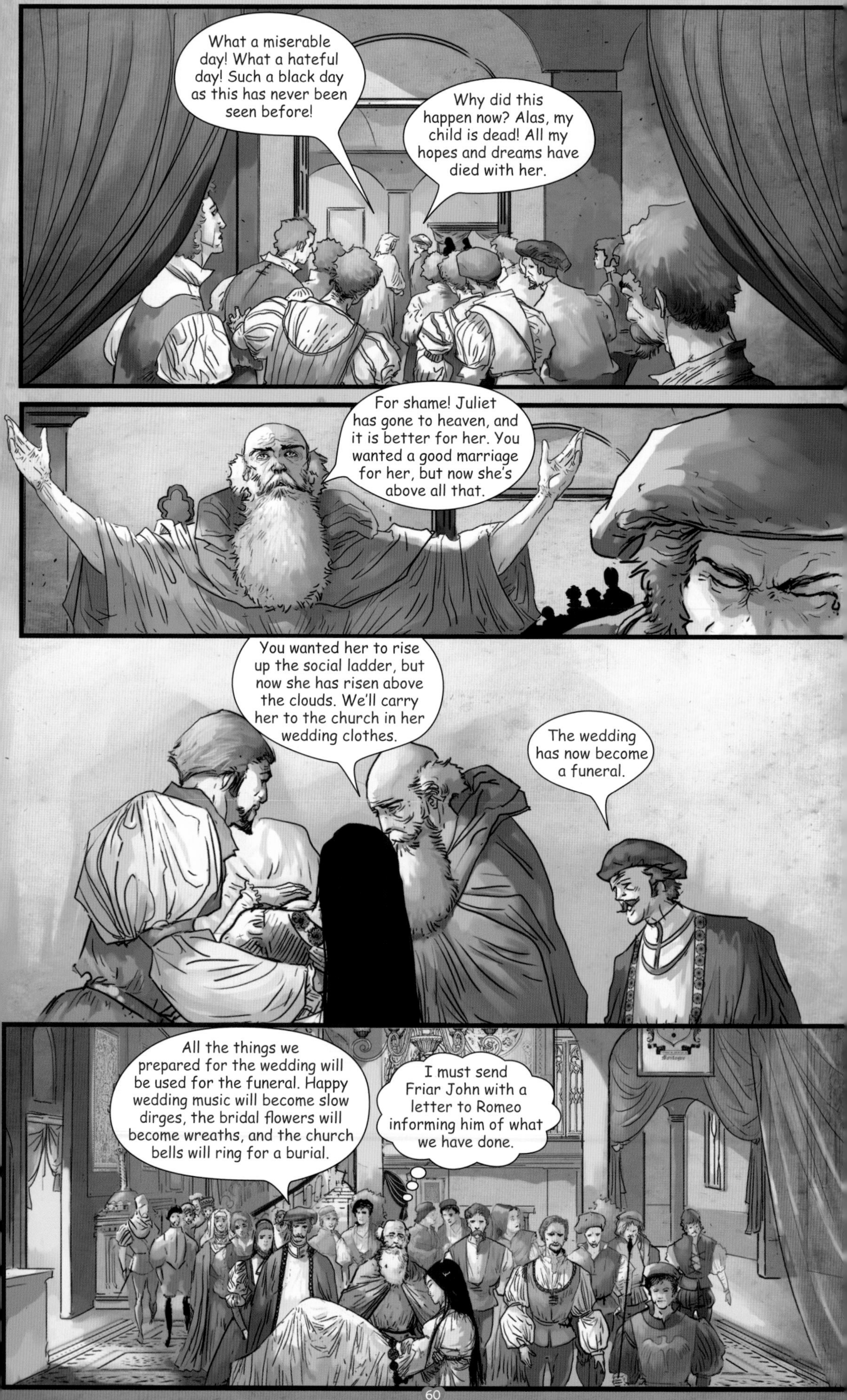
What a miserable day! What a hateful day! Such a black day as this has never been seen before!
Why did this happen now? Alas, my child is dead! All my hopes and dreams have died with her.
For shame! Juliet has gone to heaven, and it is better for her. You wanted a good marriage for her, but now she's above all that.
You wanted her to rise up the social ladder, but now she has risen above the clouds. We'll carry her to the church in her wedding clothes.
The wedding has now become a funeral.
All the things we prepared for the wedding will be used for the funeral. Happy wedding music will become slow dirges, the bridal flowers will become wreaths, and the church bells will ring for a burial.
I must send Friar John with a letter to Romeo informing him of what we have done.

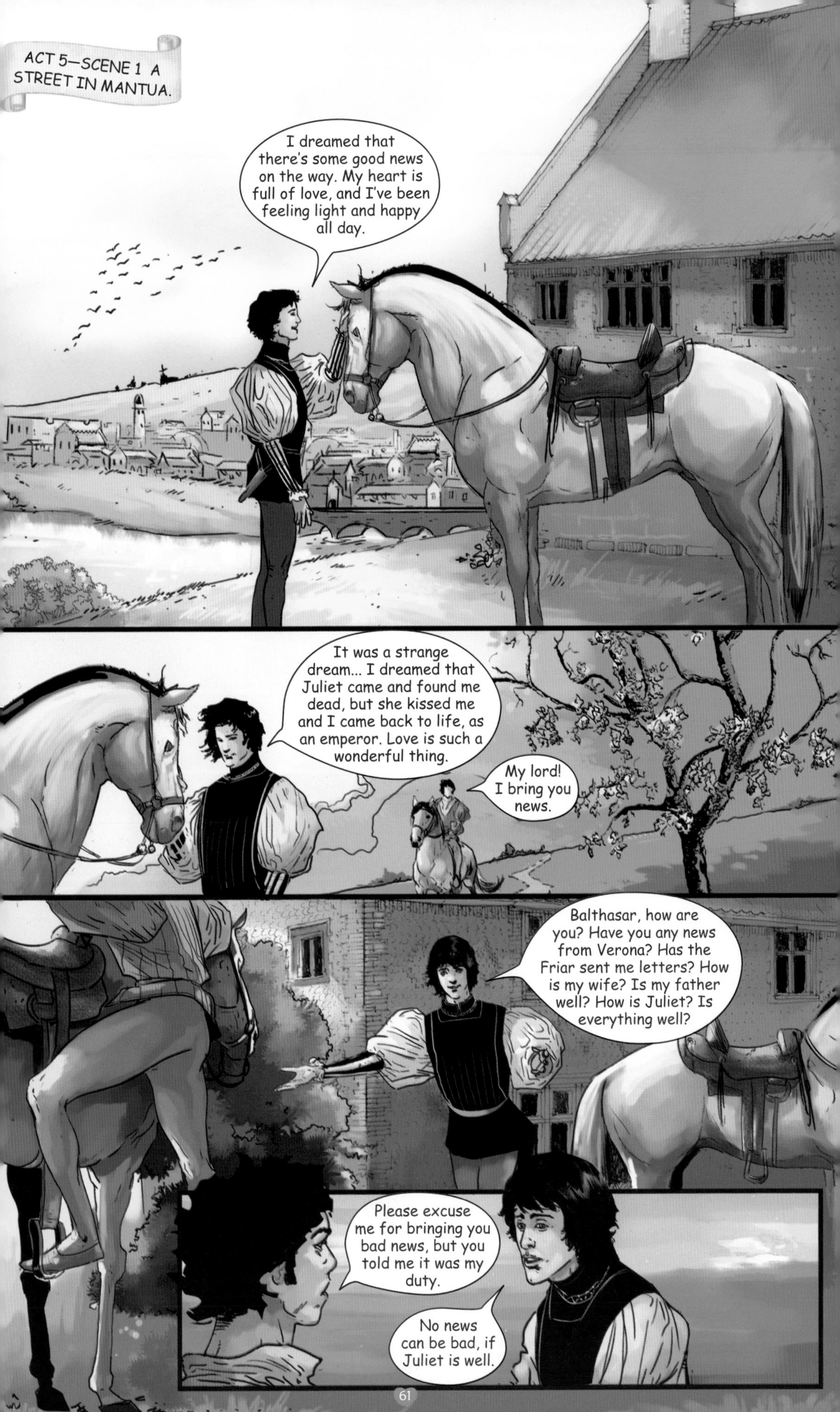
ACT 5—SCENE 1 A STREET IN MANTUA.
I dreamed that there's some good news on the way. My heart is full of love, and I've been feeling light and happy all day.
It was a strange dream... I dreamed that Juliet came and found me dead, but she kissed me and I came back to life, as an emperor. Love is such a wonderful thing.
My lord! I bring you news.
Balthasar, how are you? Have you any news from Verona? Has the Friar sent me letters? How is my wife? Is my father well? How is Juliet? Is everything well?
Please excuse me for bringing you bad news, but you told me it was my duty.
No news can be bad, if Juliet is well.

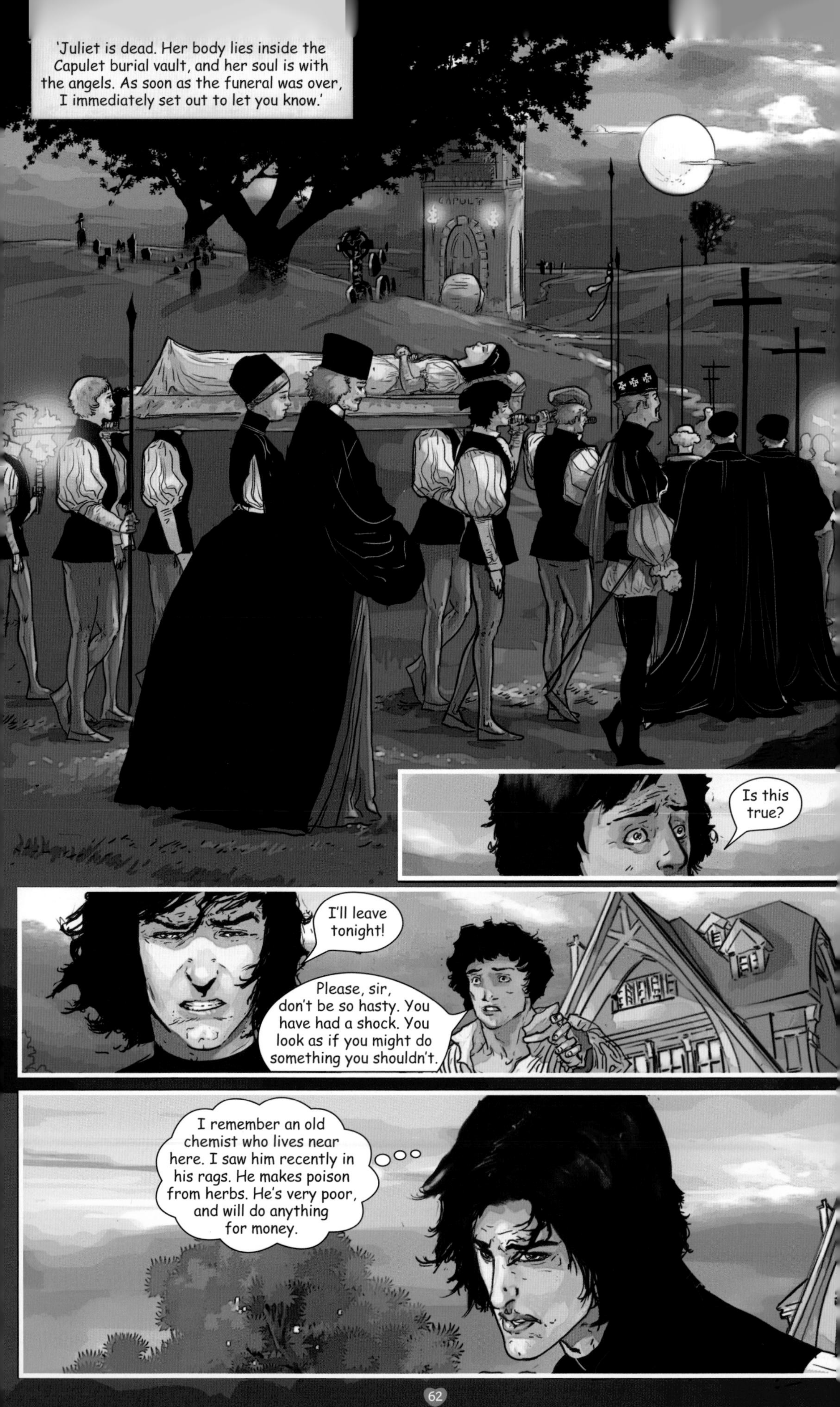
'Juliet is dead. Her body lies inside the Capulet burial vault, and her soul is with the angels. As soon as the funeral was over, I immediately set out to let you know.'
CAPULET
Is this true?
I'll leave tonight!
Please, sir, don't be so hasty. You have had a shock. You look as if you might do something you shouldn't.
I remember an old chemist who lives near here. I saw him recently in his rags. He makes poison from herbs. He's very poor, and will do anything for money.

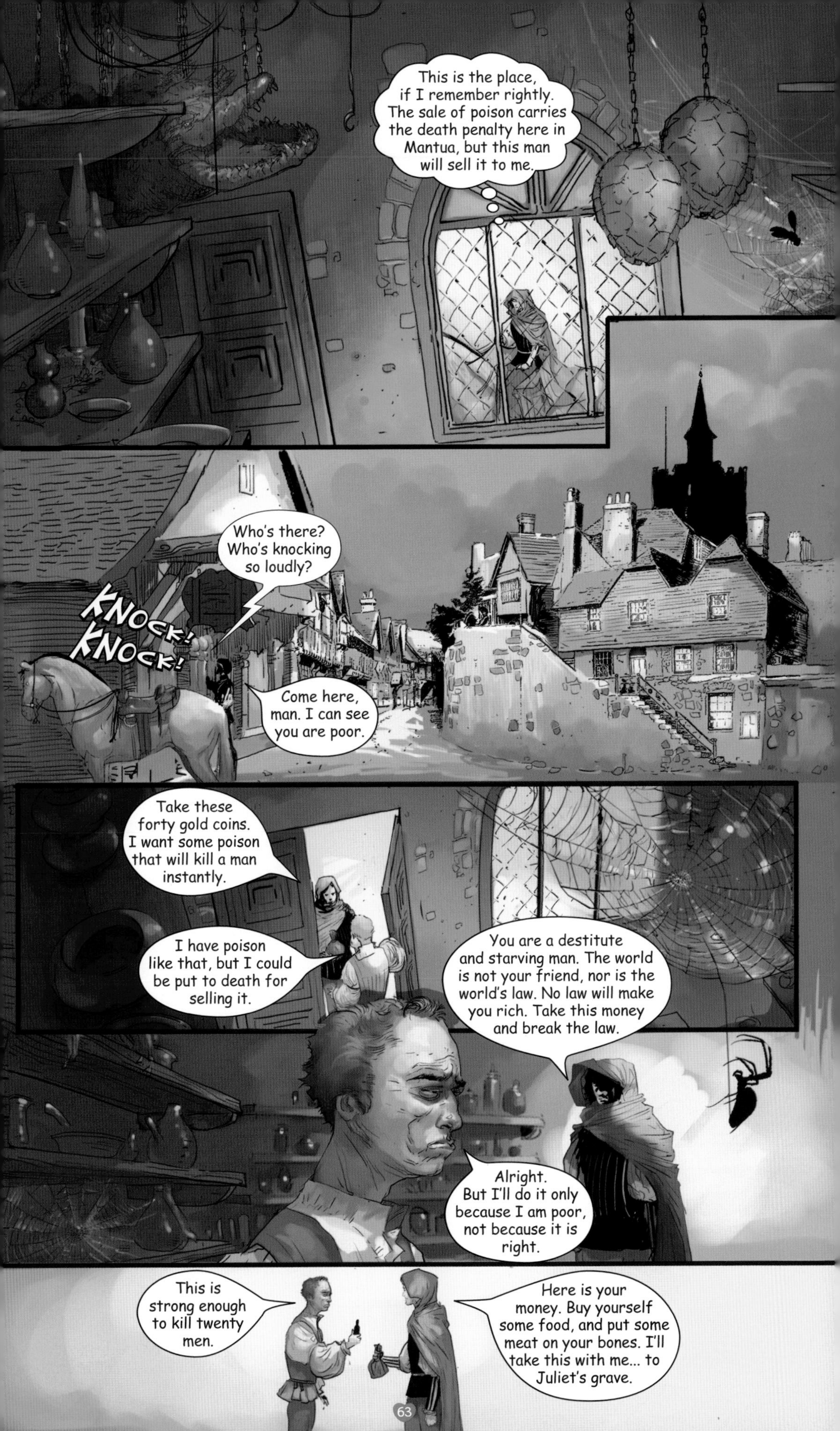
This is the place, if I remember rightly. The sale of poison carries the death penalty here in Mantua, but this man will sell it to me.
KNOCK! KNOCK!
Who's there? Who's knocking so loudly?
Come here, man. I can see you are poor.
Take these forty gold coins. I want some poison that will kill a man instantly.
I have poison like that, but I could be put to death for selling it.
You are a destitute and starving man. The world is not your friend, nor is the world's law. No law will make you rich. Take this money and break the law.
Alright. But I'll do it only because I am poor, not because it is right.
This is strong enough to kill twenty men.
Here is your money. Buy yourself some food, and put some meat on your bones. I'll take this with me... to Juliet's grave.

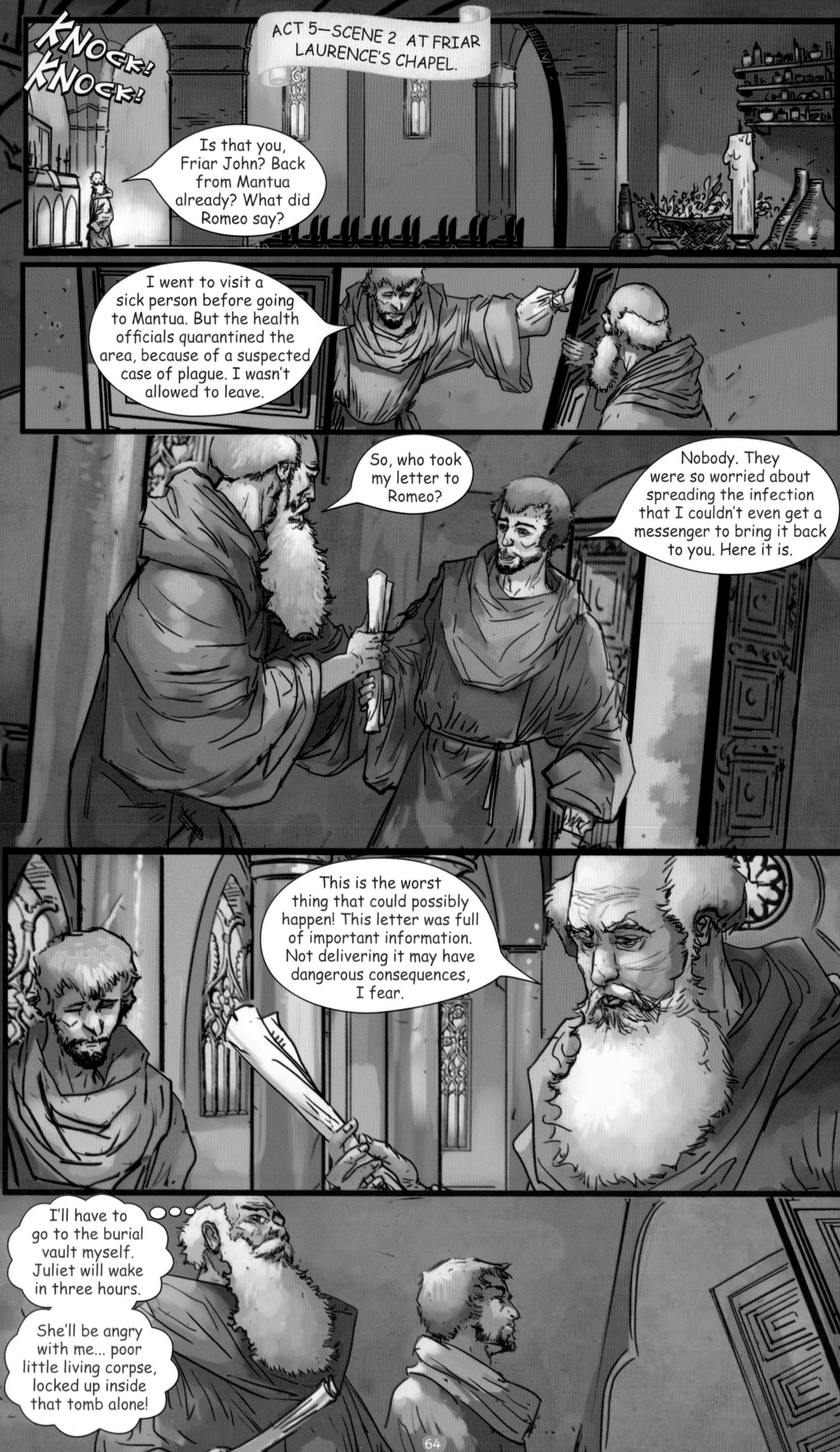
KNOCK! KNOCK!
ACT 5—SCENE 2 AT FRIAR LAURENCE'S CHAPEL.
Is that you, Friar John? Back from Mantua already? What did Romeo say?
I went to visit a sick person before going to Mantua. But the health officials quarantined the area, because of a suspected case of plague. I wasn't allowed to leave.
So, who took my letter to Romeo?
Nobody. They were so worried about spreading the infection that I couldn't even get a messenger to bring it back to you. Here it is.
This is the worst thing that could possibly happen! This letter was full of important information. Not delivering it may have dangerous consequences, I fear.
I'll have to go to the burial vault myself. Juliet will wake in three hours.
She'll be angry with me... poor little living corpse, locked up inside that tomb alone!

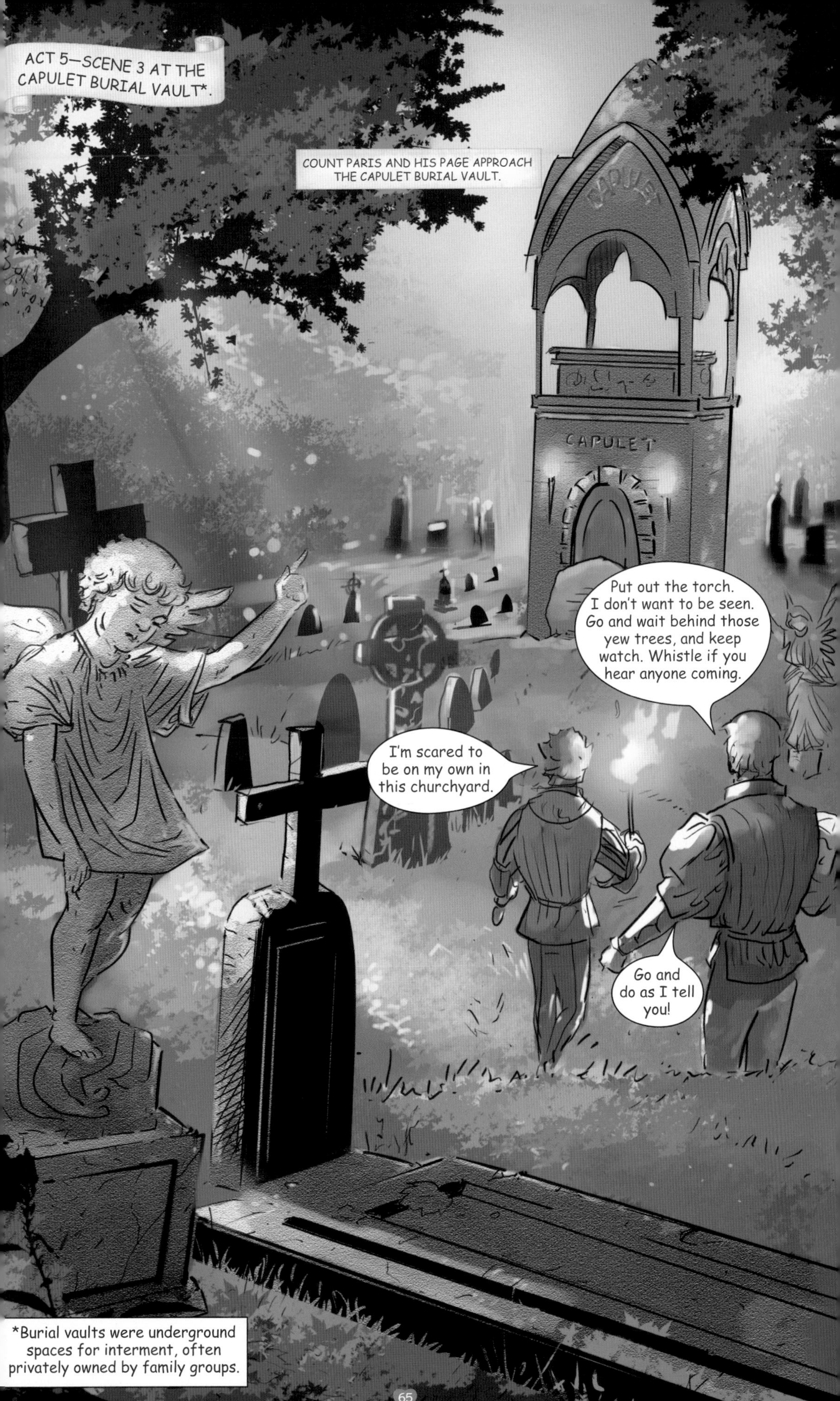
ACT 5—SCENE 3 AT THE CAPULET BURIAL VAULT*.
COUNT PARIS AND HIS PAGE APPROACH THE CAPULET BURIAL VAULT.
CAPULET
Put out the torch. I don't want to be seen. Go and wait behind those yew trees, and keep watch. Whistle if you hear anyone coming.
I'm scared to be on my own in this churchyard.
Go and do as I tell you!
*Burial vaults were underground spaces for interment, often privately owned by family groups.

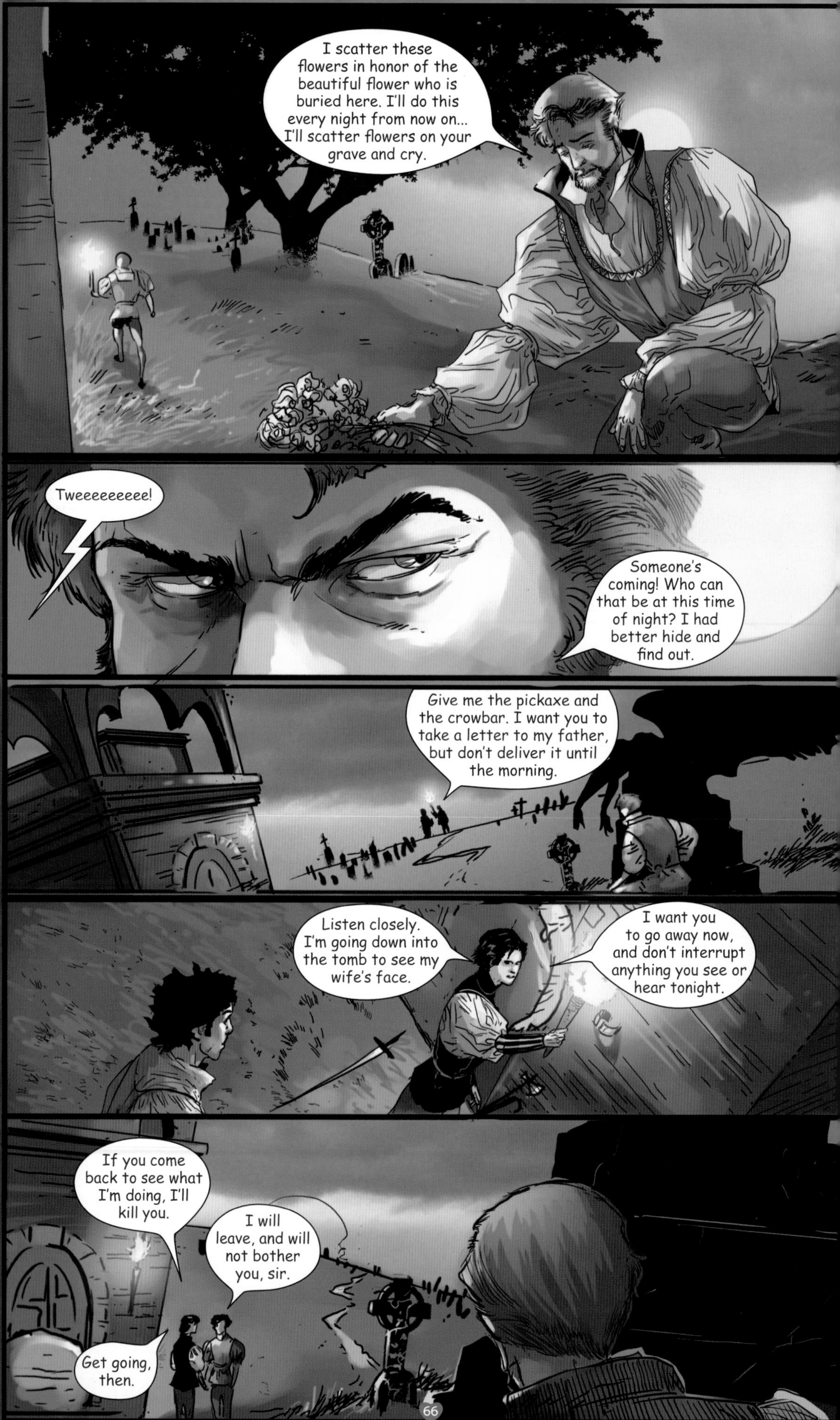
I scatter these flowers in honor of the beautiful flower who is buried here. I'll do this every night from now on... I'll scatter flowers on your grave and cry.
Tweeeeeeeee!
Someone's coming! Who can that be at this time of night? I had better hide and find out.
Give me the pickaxe and the crowbar. I want you to take a letter to my father, but don't deliver it until the morning.
Listen closely. I'm going down into the tomb to see my wife's face.
I want you to go away now, and don't interrupt anything you see or hear tonight.
If you come back to see what I'm doing, I'll kill you.
I will leave, and will not bother you, sir.
Get going, then.

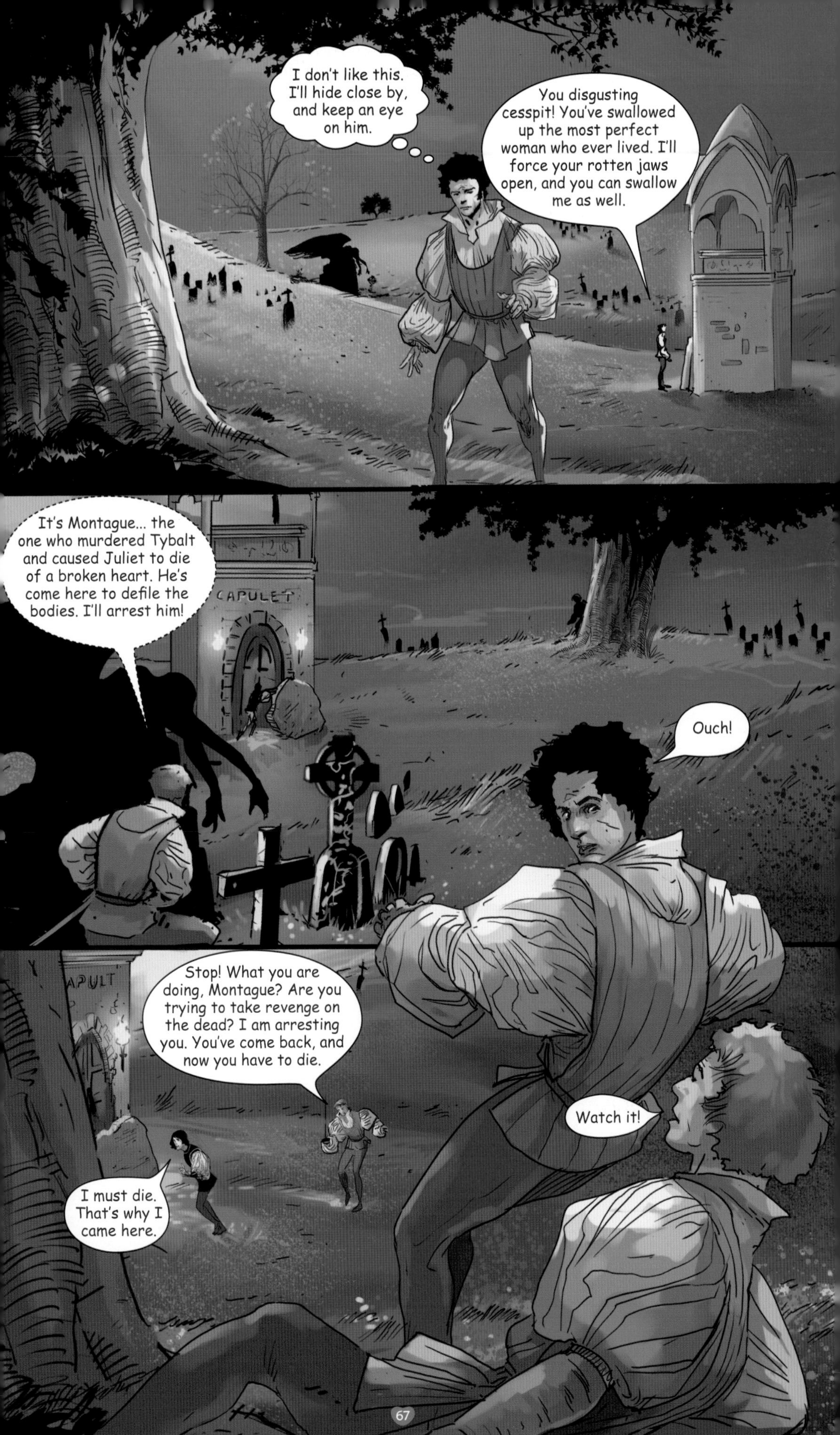
I don't like this. I'll hide close by, and keep an eye on him.
You disgusting cesspit! You've swallowed up the most perfect woman who ever lived. I'll force your rotten jaws open, and you can swallow me as well.
It's Montague... the one who murdered Tybalt and caused Juliet to die of a broken heart. He's come here to defile the bodies. I'll arrest him!
CAPULET
Ouch!
APULT
Stop! What you are doing, Montague? Are you trying to take revenge on the dead? I am arresting you. You've come back, and now you have to die.
Watch it!
I must die. That's why I came here.

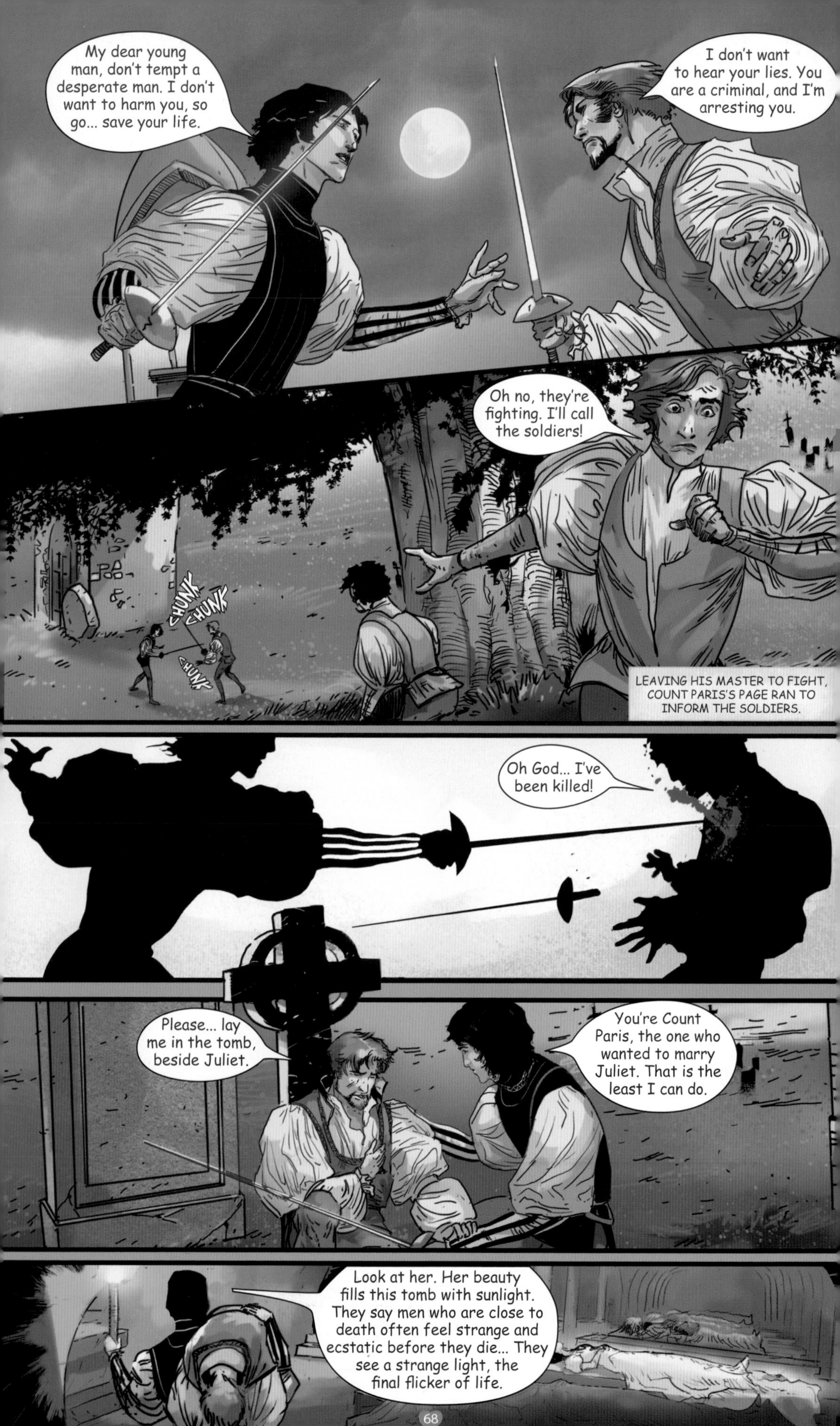

My dear young man, don't tempt a desperate man. I don't want to harm you, so go... save your life.
I don't want to hear your lies. You are a criminal, and I'm arresting you.
Oh no, they're fighting. I'll call the soldiers!
CHUNK
CHUNK
CHUNK
LEAVING HIS MASTER TO FIGHT, COUNT PARIS'S PAGE RAN TO INFORM THE SOLDIERS.
Oh God... I've been killed!
Please... lay me in the tomb, beside Juliet.
You're Count Paris, the one who wanted to marry Juliet. That is the least I can do.
Look at her. Her beauty fills this tomb with sunlight. They say men who are close to death often feel strange and ecstatic before they die... They see a strange light, the final flicker of life.

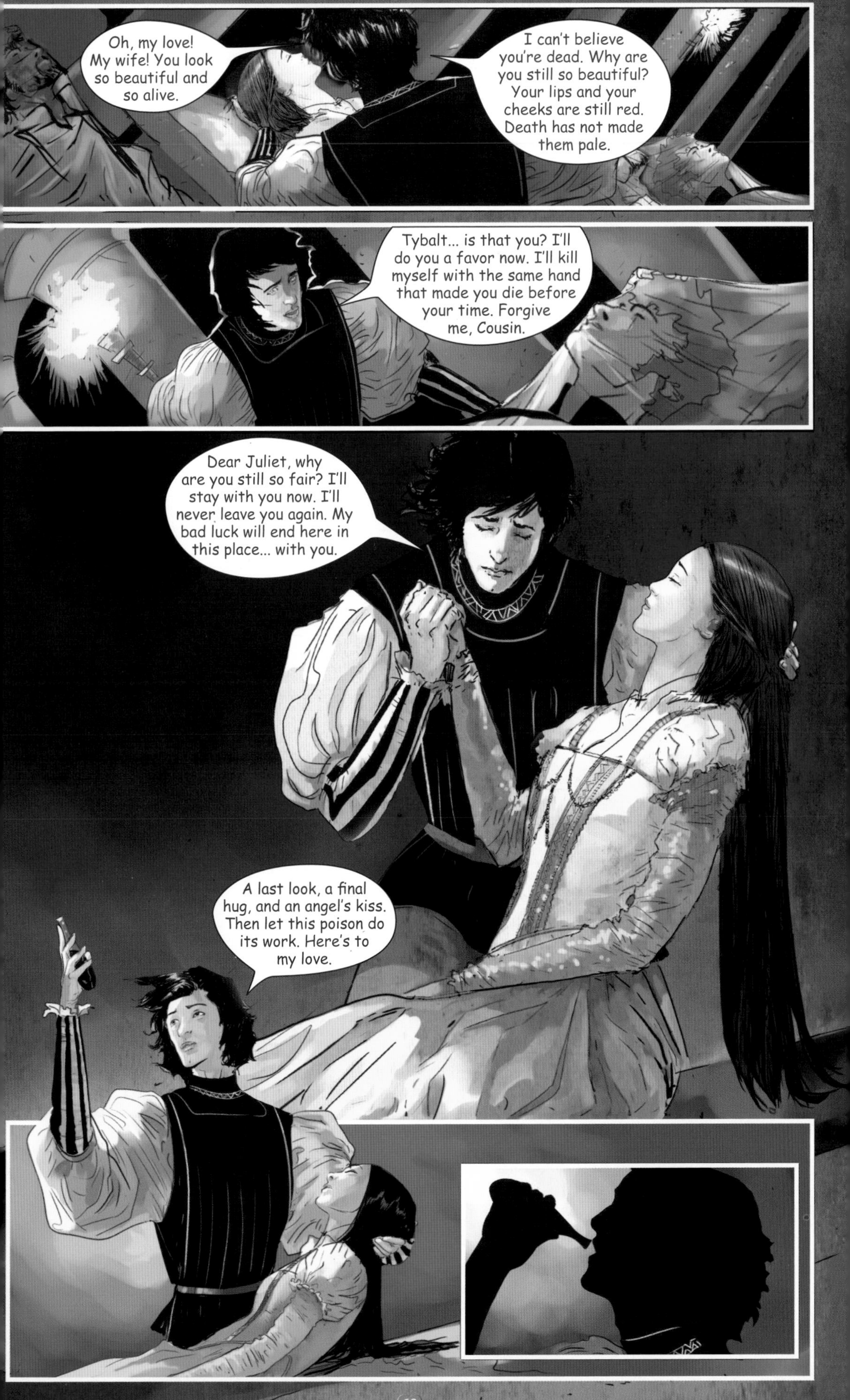
Oh, my love! My wife! You look so beautiful and so alive.
I can't believe you're dead. Why are you still so beautiful? Your lips and your cheeks are still red. Death has not made them pale.
Tybalt... is that you? I'll do you a favor now. I'll kill myself with the same hand that made you die before your time. Forgive me, Cousin.
Dear Juliet, why are you still so fair? I'll stay with you now. I'll never leave you again. My bad luck will end here in this place... with you.
A last look, a final hug, and an angel's kiss. Then let this poison do its work. Here's to my love.

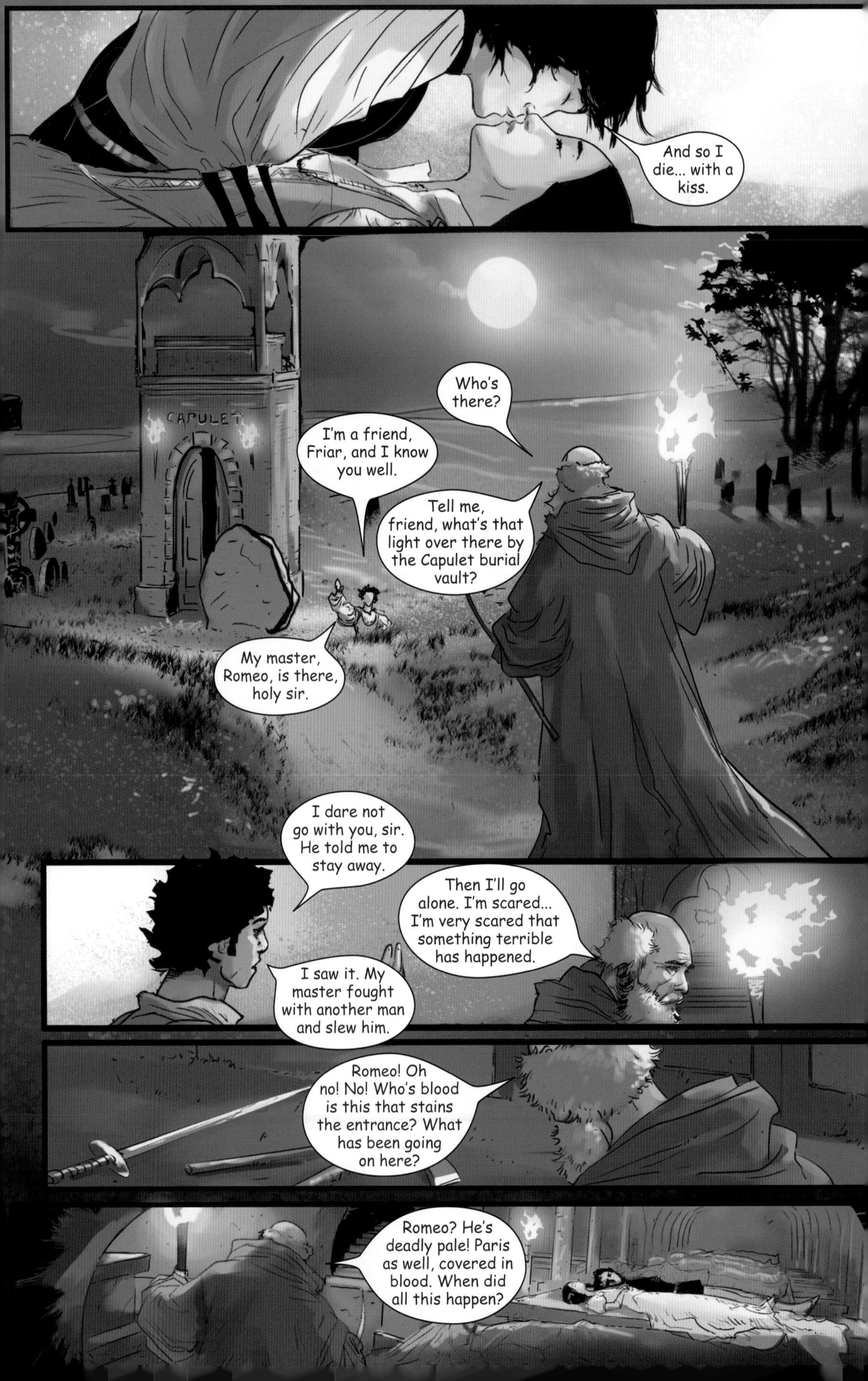
And so I die... with a kiss.
Who's there?
I'm a friend, Friar, and I know you well.
Tell me, friend, what's that light over there by the Capulet burial vault?
CAPULET
My master, Romeo, is there, holy sir.
I dare not go with you, sir. He told me to stay away.
Then I'll go alone. I'm scared... I'm very scared that something terrible has happened.
I saw it. My master fought with another man and slew him.
Romeo! Oh no! No! Who's blood is this that stains the entrance? What has been going on here?
Romeo? He's deadly pale! Paris as well, covered in blood. When did all this happen?

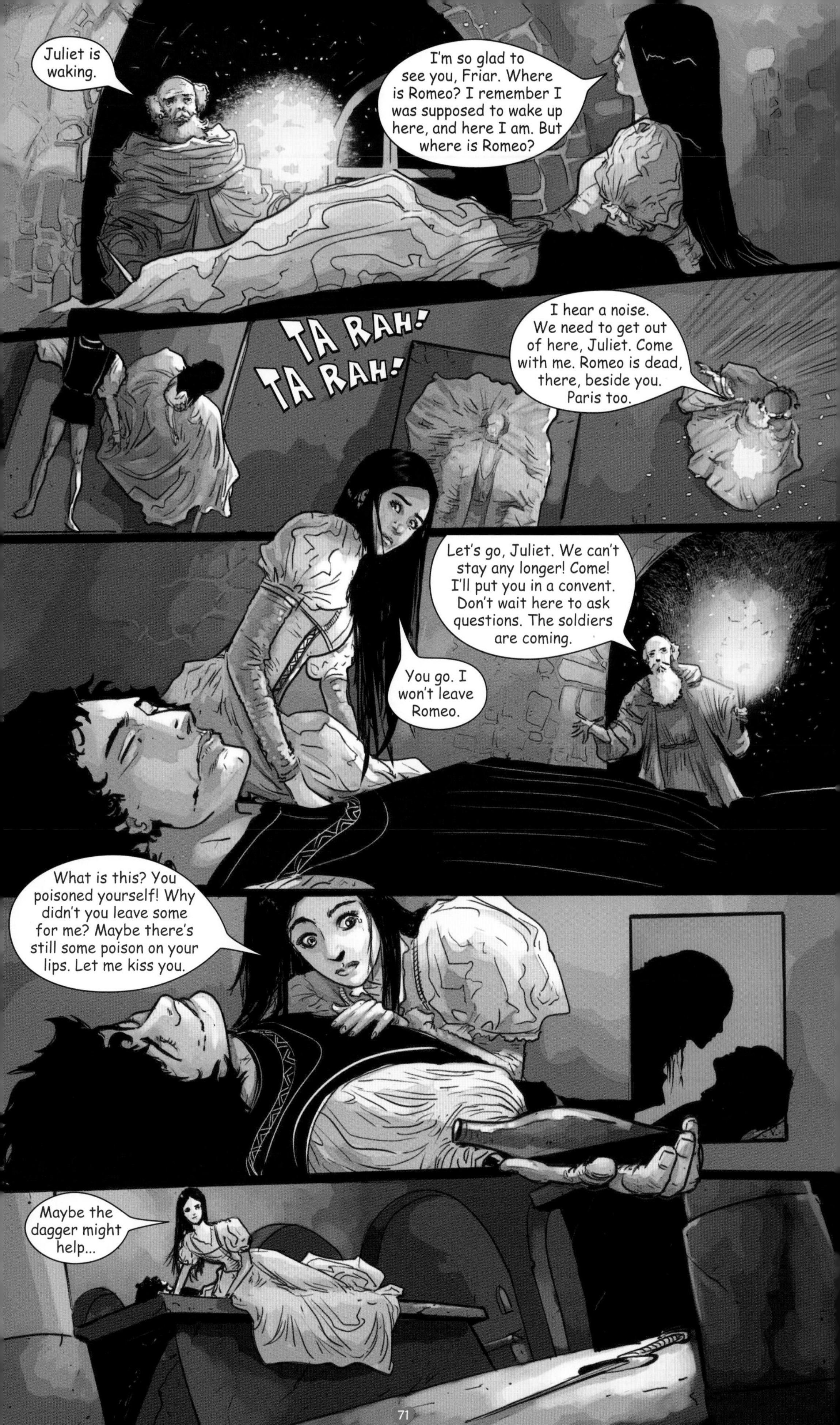
Juliet is waking.
I'm so glad to see you, Friar. Where is Romeo? I remember I was supposed to wake up here, and here I am. But where is Romeo?
TA RAH! TA RAH!
I hear a noise. We need to get out of here, Juliet. Come with me. Romeo is dead, there, beside you. Paris too.
Let's go, Juliet. We can't stay any longer! Come! I'll put you in a convent. Don't wait here to ask questions. The soldiers are coming.
You go. I won't leave Romeo.
What is this? You poisoned yourself! Why didn't you leave some for me? Maybe there's still some poison on your lips. Let me kiss you.
Maybe the dagger might help...

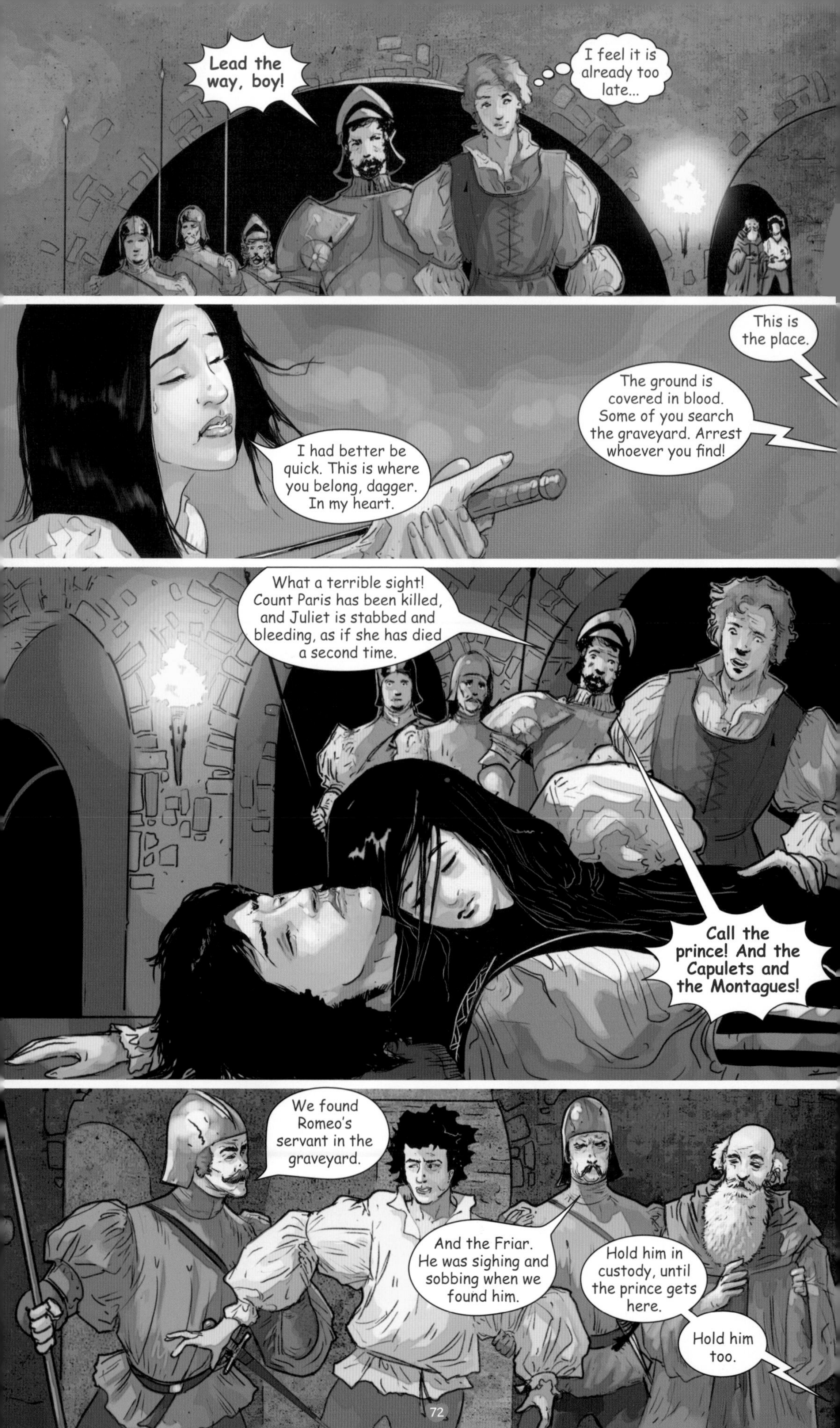
Lead the way, boy!
I feel it is already too late...
I had better be quick. This is where you belong, dagger. In my heart.
This is the place.
The ground is covered in blood. Some of you search the graveyard. Arrest whoever you find!
What a terrible sight! Count Paris has been killed, and Juliet is stabbed and bleeding, as if she has died a second time.
Call the prince! And the Capulets and the Montagues!
We found Romeo's servant in the graveyard.
And the Friar. He was sighing and sobbing when we found him.
Hold him in custody, until the prince gets here.
Hold him too.

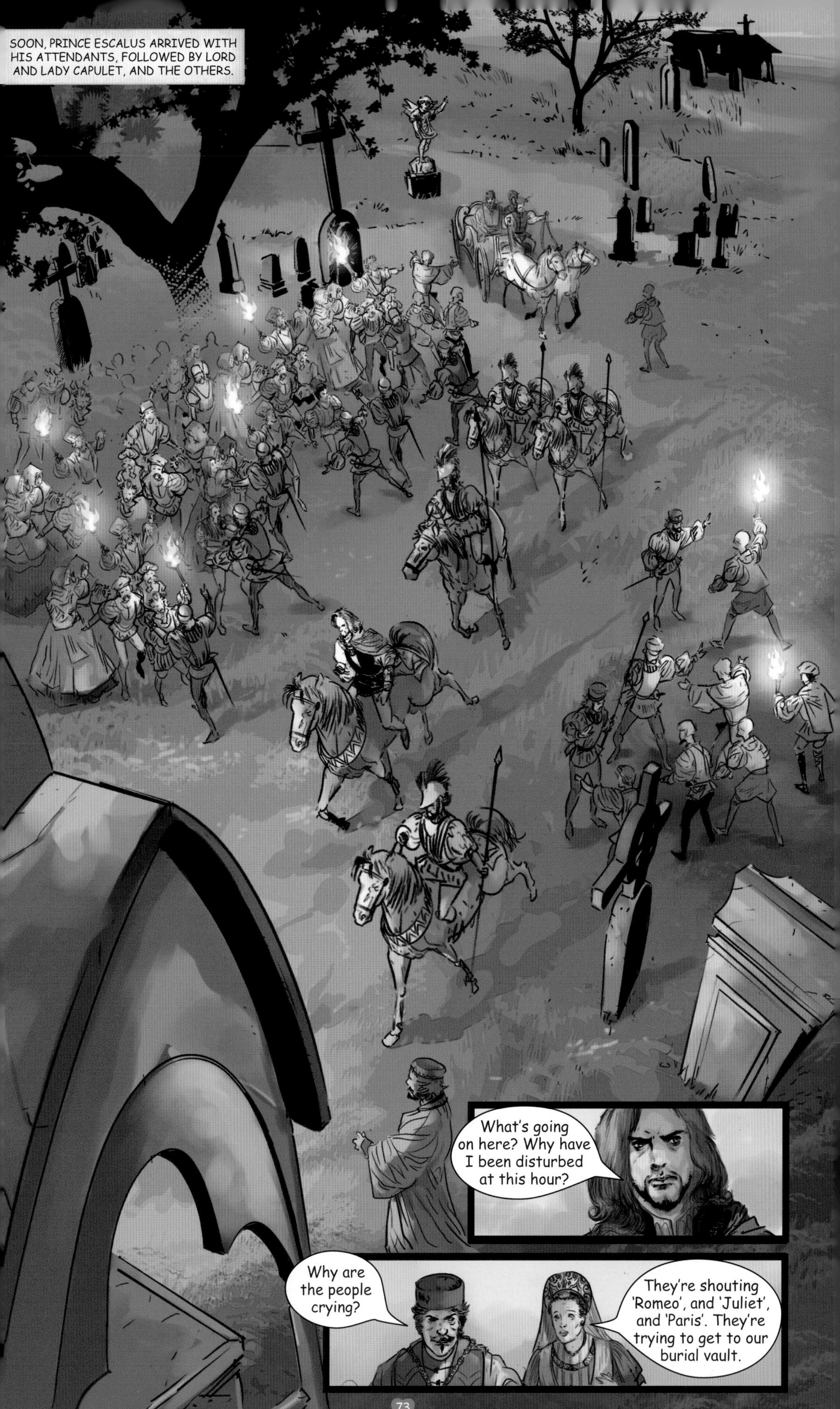
SOON, PRINCE ESCALUS ARRIVED WITH HIS ATTENDANTS, FOLLOWED BY LORD AND LADY CAPULET, AND THE OTHERS.
What's going on here? Why have I been disturbed at this hour?
Why are the people crying?
They're shouting 'Romeo', and 'Juliet', and 'Paris'. They're trying to get to our burial vault.

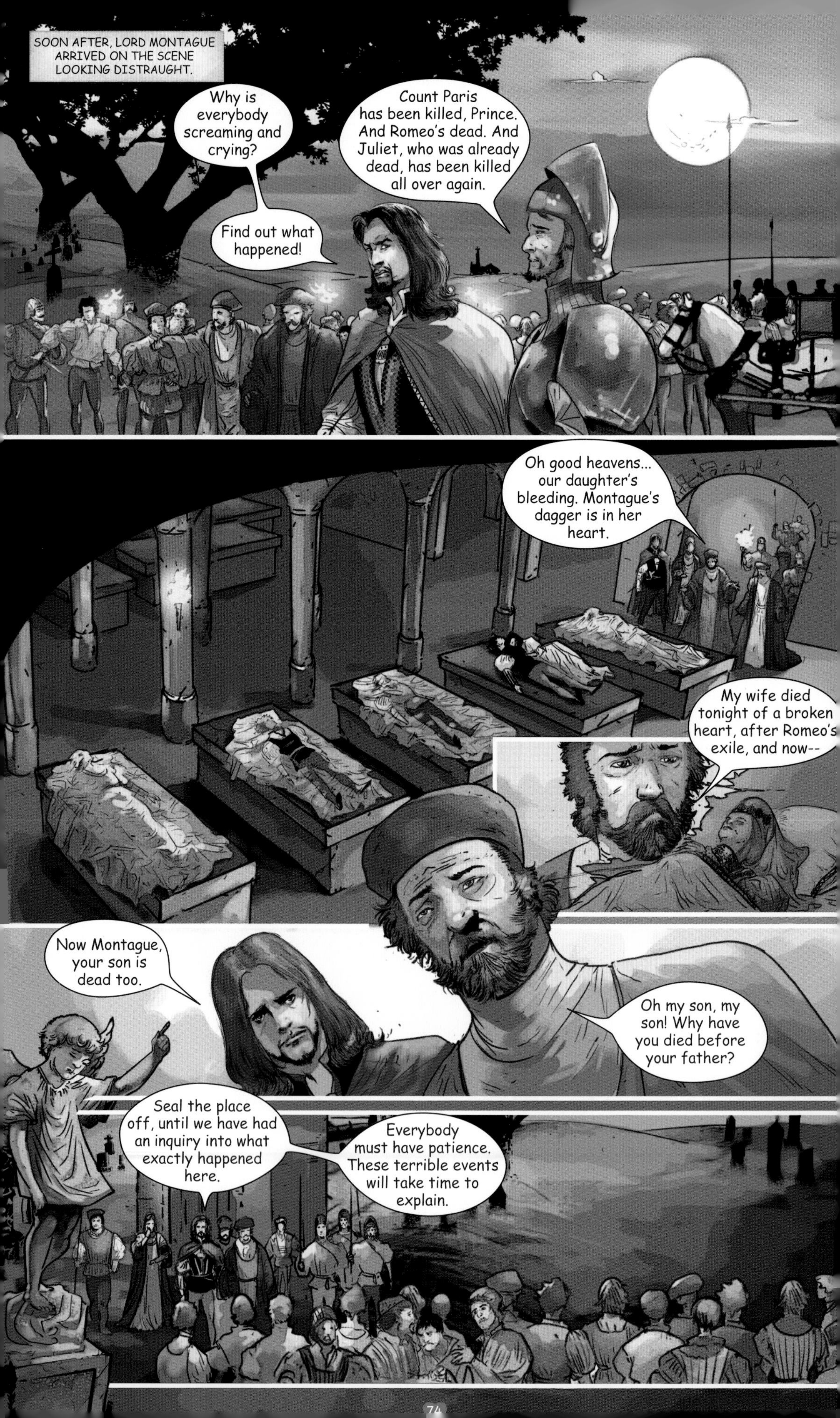
SOON AFTER, LORD MONTAGUE ARRIVED ON THE SCENE LOOKING DISTRAUGHT.
Why is everybody screaming and crying?
Find out what happened!
Count Paris has been killed, Prince. And Romeo's dead. And Juliet, who was already dead, has been killed all over again.
Oh good heavens... our daughter's bleeding. Montague's dagger is in her heart.
My wife died tonight of a broken heart, after Romeo's exile, and now--
Now Montague, your son is dead too.
Oh my son, my son! Why have you died before your father?
Seal the place off, until we have had an inquiry into what exactly happened here.
Everybody must have patience. These terrible events will take time to explain.

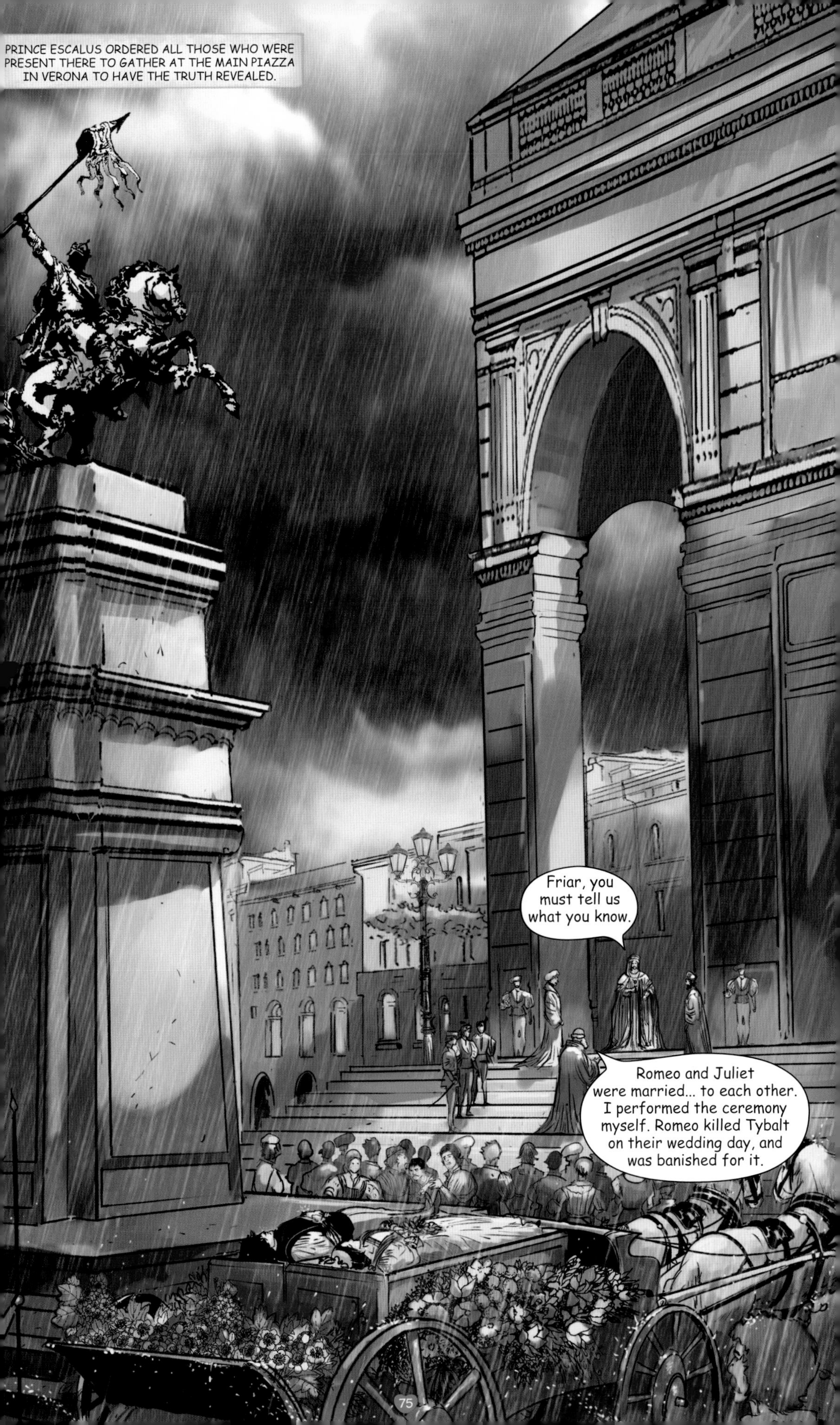
PRINCE ESCALUS ORDERED ALL THOSE WHO WERE PRESENT THERE TO GATHER AT THE MAIN PIAZZA IN VERONA TO HAVE THE TRUTH REVEALED.
Friar, you must tell us what you know.
Romeo and Juliet were married... to each other. I performed the ceremony myself. Romeo killed Tybalt on their wedding day, and was banished for it.

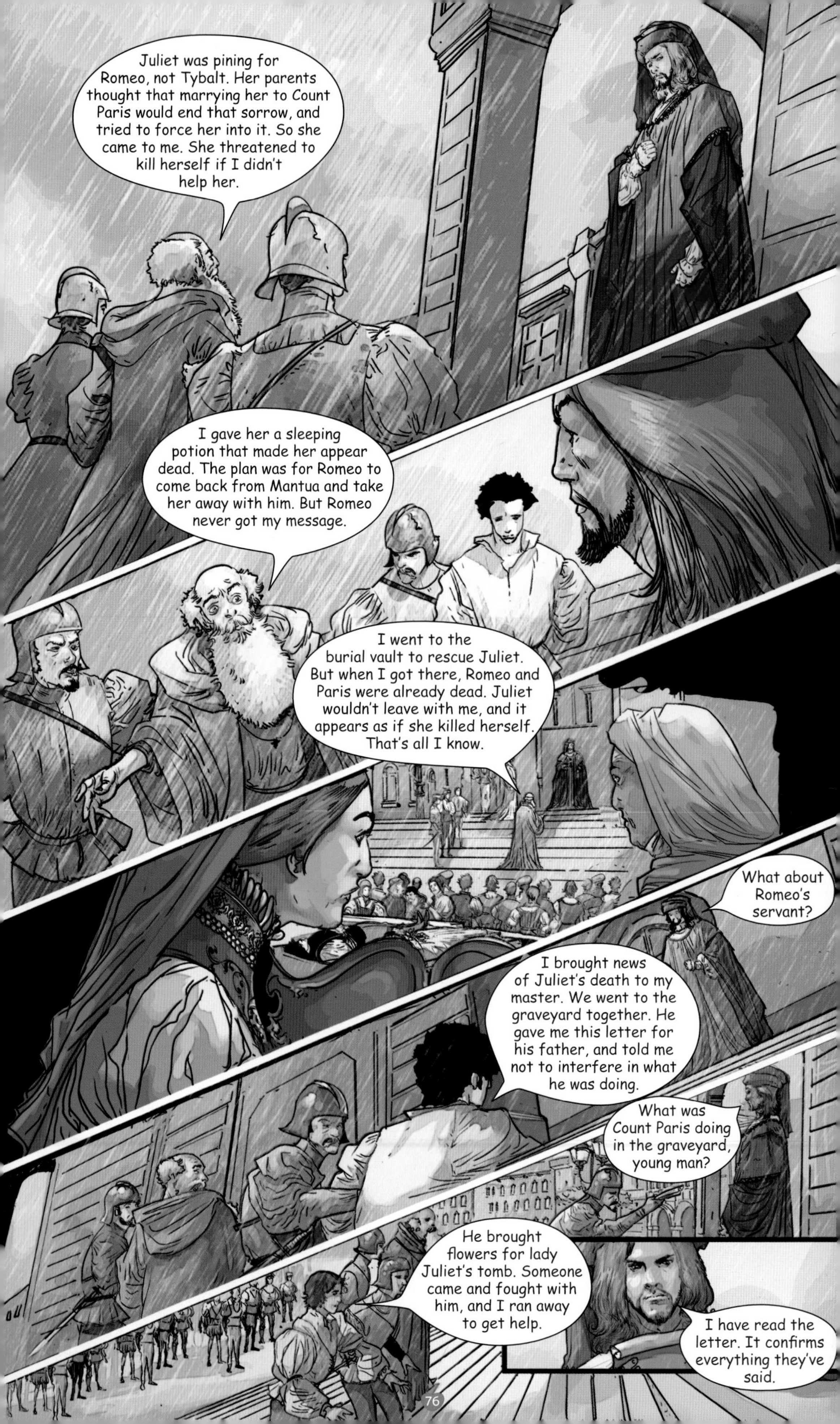
Juliet was pining for Romeo, not Tybalt. Her parents thought that marrying her to Count Paris would end that sorrow, and tried to force her into it. So she came to me. She threatened to kill herself if I didn't help her.
I gave her a sleeping potion that made her appear dead. The plan was for Romeo to come back from Mantua and take her away with him. But Romeo never got my message.
I went to the burial vault to rescue Juliet. But when I got there, Romeo and Paris were already dead. Juliet wouldn't leave with me, and it appears as if she killed herself. That's all I know.
What about Romeo's servant?
I brought news of Juliet's death to my master. We went to the graveyard together. He gave me this letter for his father, and told me not to interfere in what he was doing.
What was Count Paris doing in the graveyard, young man?
He brought flowers for lady Juliet's tomb. Someone came and fought with him, and I ran away to get help.
I have read the letter. It confirms everything they've said.

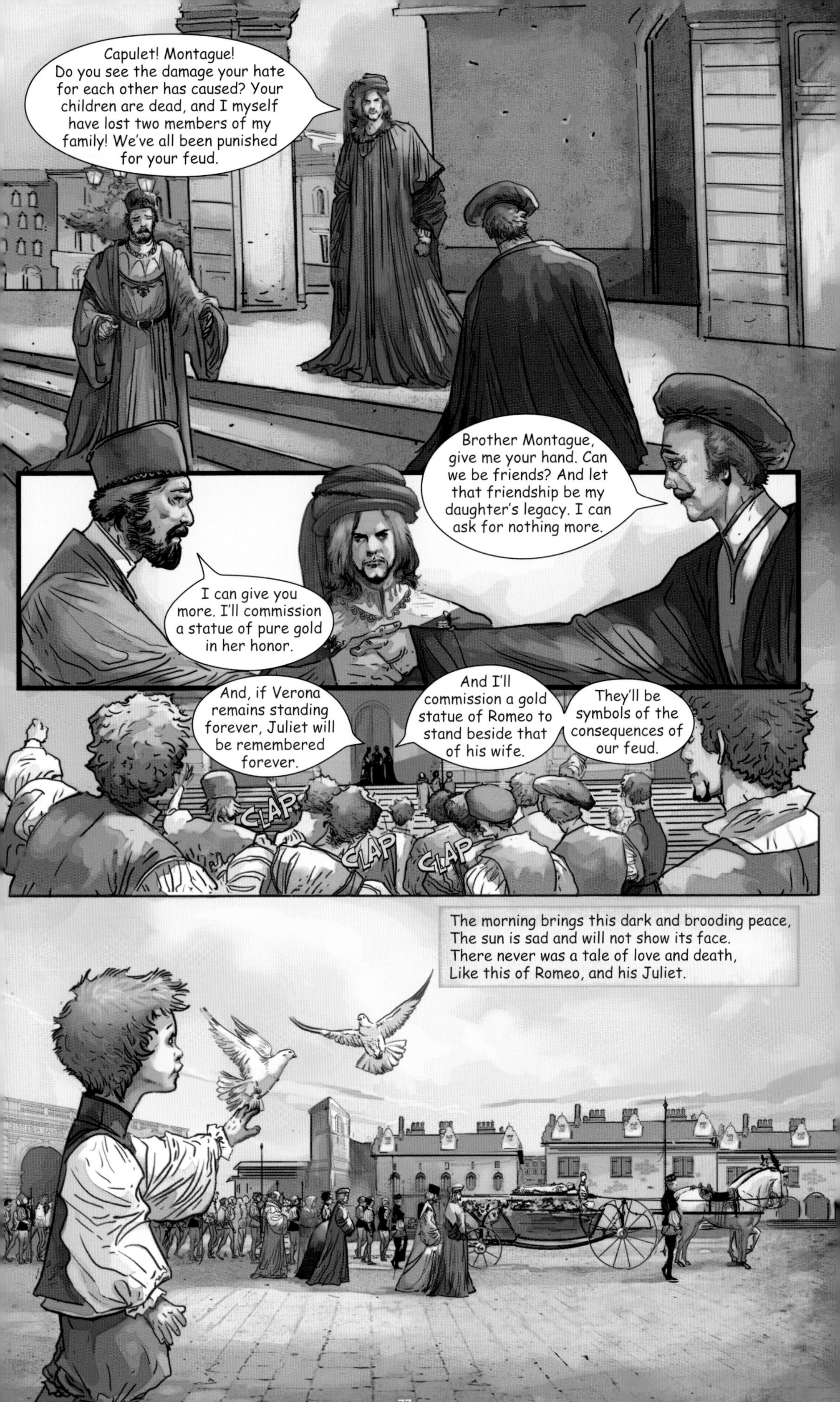
Capulet! Montague! Do you see the damage your hate for each other has caused? Your children are dead, and I myself have lost two members of my family! We've all been punished for your feud.
Brother Montague, give me your hand. Can we be friends? And let that friendship be my daughter's legacy. I can ask for nothing more.
I can give you more. I'll commission a statue of pure gold in her honor.
And, if Verona remains standing forever, Juliet will be remembered forever.
And I'll commission a gold statue of Romeo to stand beside that of his wife.
They'll be symbols of the consequences of our feud.
CLAP
CLAP
CLAP
The morning brings this dark and brooding peace,
The sun is sad and will not show its face.
There never was a tale of love and death,
Like this of Romeo, and his Juliet.

THE PLAYWRIGHT AND THE PLAY

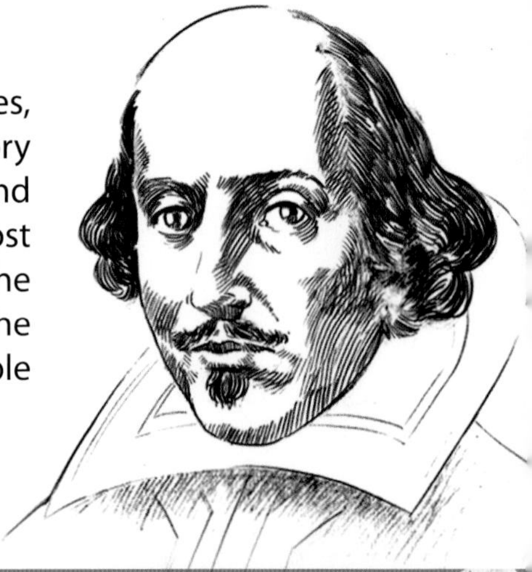

Transcending time, cultures, and languages, ***Romeo and Juliet*** is the most famous love story in the world. The man behind it all—the one and only William Shakespeare—was one of the most interesting and mysterious playwrights in the world. Other than the queen, the Big Ben, and the red buses, Shakespeare is the most identifiable icon of England!

You've probably heard of him but do you know that:

- Shakespeare is responsible for over 1700 words that we use everyday. He was the first person to use words like 'aerial', 'majestic', 'road', 'lonely', and 'laughable' among many more. If you think you don't know Shakespeare, think again! Have you ever said phrases like 'All that glitters is not gold' or 'It's all Greek to me'? Well, those are his creations!
- Shakespeare, the greatest icon that literature has known, never went to university.
- Shakespeare never published any of his plays. We read his plays today only because his fellow actors John Hemminges and Henry Condell recorded his work after he died, as a tribute to him. They compiled a collection known as the *First Folio*. This is the source from which all published Shakespeare books are derived. It is also an important proof that he authored his plays.
- Nobody knows what Shakespeare was up to between 1585 to 1592!

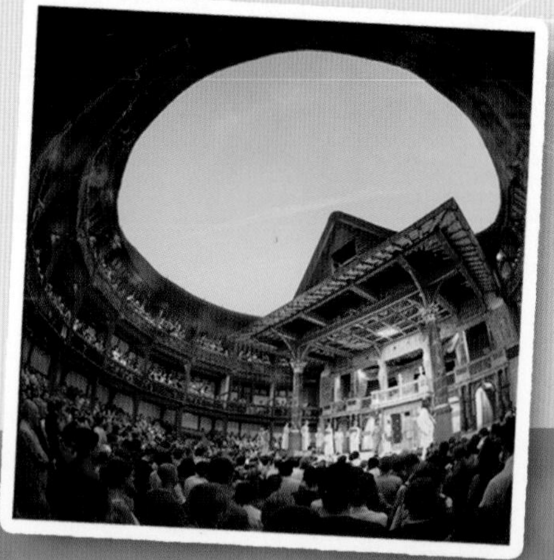

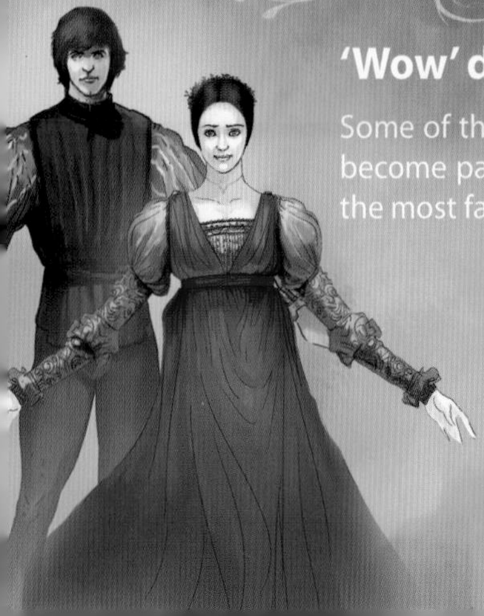

'Wow' dialogs from the play

Some of the dialogs in the play are oft-quoted and have become part of popular culture. Have a look at some of the most famous of them:

- ***What is in a name? That which we call a rose, By any other name would be as sweet.***
- ***Good night, good night! Parting is such sweet sorrow, That I shall say good night till it be morrow.***
- ***Oh Romeo, Romeo, wherefort art thou Romeo?***

And the story lives on...

The story of *Romeo and Juliet* lives on till today. Don't believe it? Listen to the young pop icon, Taylor Swift's *Love Story* and you'd know what we mean! The song is a modernized version of the classic story and went on to become a number one hit on music charts across the world.

TAYLOR
SWIFT
Love
Story

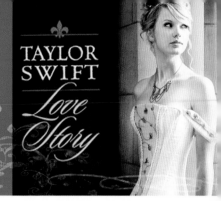

THE BALCONY SCENE

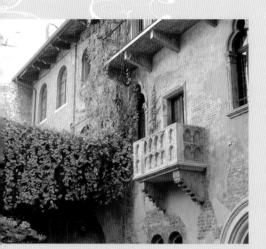

Perhaps one of the most famous scenes of Shakespeare's plays is the balcony scene in *Romeo and Juliet*. The scene is set in a garden in Verona, Italy. The house you're seeing is believed to be the real home of Juliet's family (the Capulets). The 13th-century building has become a much sought-after tourist site. In the real-life garden, there is a statue of Juliet in the courtyard near the balcony where Romeo is believed to have serenaded her.

Did you know?

Two new
outer rings
R1
U2
Miranda
New moon,
Mab
Puck
Perdita
Belinda
Cordelia
Ophelia
Bianca
Cressida
Desdemona
Juliet
Portia
Rosalind
Orbit
Ring
New moon,
Cupid

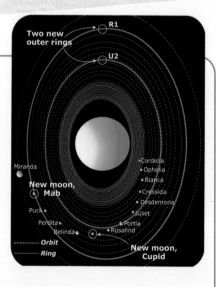

- Moons of the planet Uranus are named after characters in Shakespeare's plays. To give you an example, two moons discovered in 1787 were named Oberon and Titania, after characters in *A Midsummer Night's Dream*. A moon discovered in 1986 was named Juliet. Two moons discovered in 1997 were named Caliban and Sycorax, after characters in *The Tempest*.
- When *Romeo and Juliet* was first enacted, for many years the role of Juliet was played by a man! Women were not permitted to act in Shakespeare's time.
- *Romeo and Juliet* is the most adapted play of Shakespeare. More than 75 movies have been made on it, the most popular being the one starring Leonardo di Caprio, released in 1996, and the musical *West Side Story* which was made in 1961.
- Globe Theatre didn't just stage plays. It acted as a bear pit and a gambling house too!

Available now

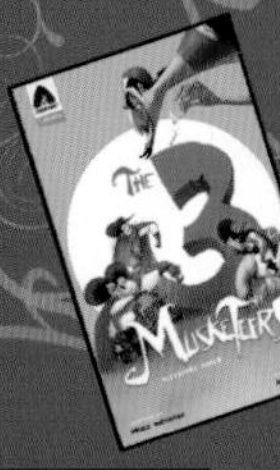

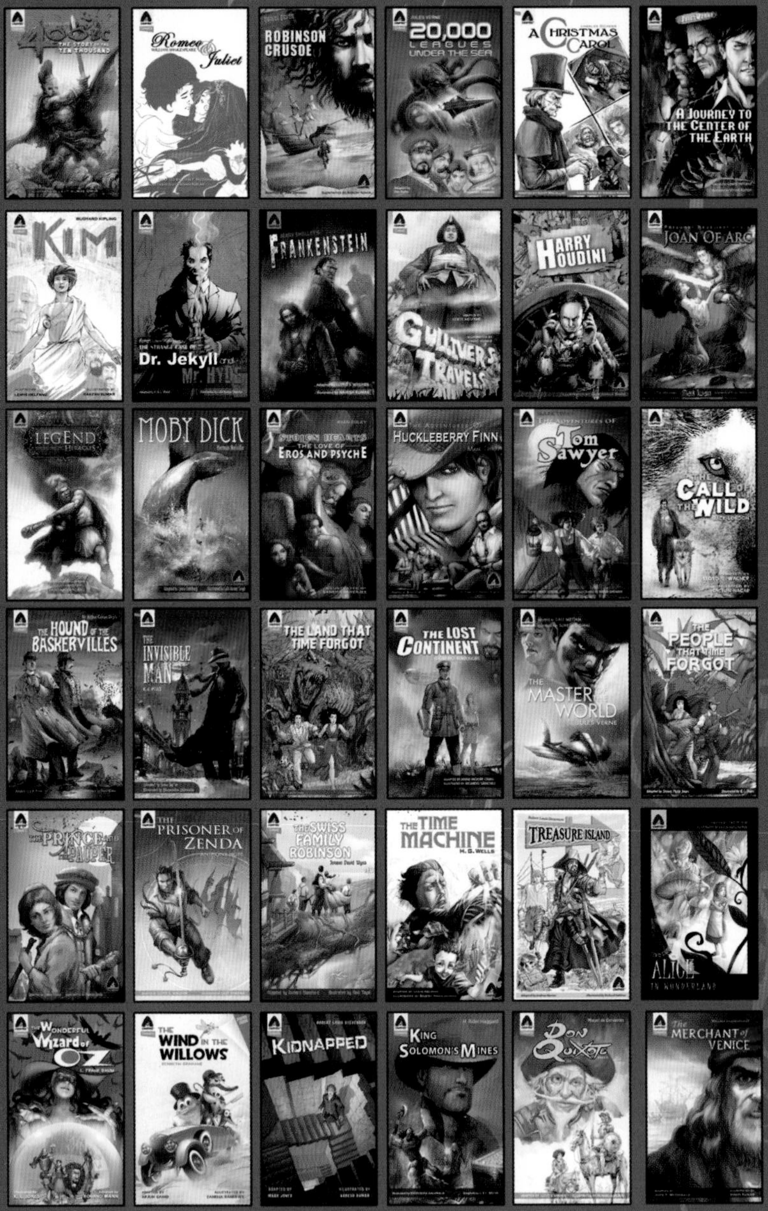
Romeo & Juliet
Robinson Crusoe
20,000 Leagues Under the Sea
A Christmas Carol
A Journey to the Center of the Earth
Kim
Dr. Jekyll
Frankenstein
Gulliver's Travels
Harry Houdini
Joan of Arc
Legend
Moby Dick
Eros and Psyche
Huckleberry Finn
Tom Sawyer
The Call of the Wild
The Hound of the Baskervilles
The Invisible Man
The Land That Time Forgot
The Lost Continent
The Master of the World
The People That Time Forgot
The Prince and the Pauper
The Prisoner of Zenda
The Swiss Family Robinson
The Time Machine
Treasure Island
Alice in Wonderland
The Wonderful Wizard of Oz
The Wind in the Willows
Kidnapped
King Solomon's Mines
Don Quixote
The Merchant of Venice

Putting the fun back into reading!

Explore the latest from Campfire at
www.campfire.co.in